Readers love Amy Lane's

Ethan in Gold

I0659687

"Amy Lane is brilliant. She knows how to weave a story that pulls on all my emotions and makes me feel like the characters are my family, my friends. I felt honored to be able to review this ARC of *Ethan in Gold.*"

—Live Your Life, Buy the Book, 5 stars

"I was at home as soon as I opened this book, I was invested in pretty much every character, and wanted to hear about where Ethan was, and who the man was that could help him get to his happy ending."

—The Tipsy Bibliophile

"*ETHAN IN GOLD* has made the Johnnies series one of my top two favourite Amy Lane series. The way it merges darkness and heartbreak with hilarious antics and heart, *ETHAN IN GOLD* shines."

—Under the Covers

"*Ethan in Gold…* is an emotionally tactile story of pain and redemption, of losing and gaining so much more in return, a story of forgiveness and absolution and of loving someone so hard, even when he doesn't believe he's loveable, that he can't help but finally understand it's not about how much he is worth but about how much he is worthy of that gift."

—The Novel Approach, 5 stars

"These guys, their issues, their love of one another, their friendship, and the hope they bring to each other will live forever and I'll keep seeing them in my dreams. Thank you, Amy, for giving me the dreams and sharing them with me."

—Rainbow Book Reviews

By AMY LANE

NOVELS
Bolt Hole
Clear Water
Gambling Men: The Novel
The Locker Room
Mourning Heaven
Racing for the Sun
Shiny!
Sidecar
A Solid Core of Alpha
The Talker Collection (anthology)
Three Fates (anthology)
Under the Rushes

THE KEEPING PROMISE ROCK SERIES
Keeping Promise Rock • Making Promises
Living Promises • Forever Promised

THE JOHNNIES SERIES
Chase in Shadow • Dex in Blue • Ethan in Gold

NOVELLAS
Bewitched by Bella's Brother
Christmas with Danny Fit
Hammer and Air
If I Must
It's Not Shakespeare
Left on St. Truth-be-Well
Puppy, Car, and Snow
Truth in the Dark
Turkey in the Snow

THE KNITTING SERIES
How to Raise an Honest Rabbit
Knitter in His Natural Habitat
Super Sock Man
The Winter Courtship Rituals of Fur-Bearing Critters

GREEN'S HILL
Guarding the Vampire's Ghost
I love you, asshole!
Litha's Constant Whim

TALKER SERIES
Talker • Talker's Redemption • Talker's Graduation

Published by DREAMSPINNER PRESS
http://www.dreamspinnerpress.com

Shiny!

AMY LANE

Dreamspinner Press

Published by
Dreamspinner Press
5032 Capital Circle SW
Suite 2, PMB# 279
Tallahassee, FL 32305-7886
USA
http://www.dreamspinnerpress.com/

Shiny!
© 2014 Amy Lane.

Cover Art
© 2014 Paul Richmond.
http://www.paulrichmondstudio.com
Cover content is for illustrative purposes only and any person depicted on the cover is a model.

ISBN: 978-1-62798-654-0
Digital ISBN: 978-1-62798-655-7

Printed in the United States of America
First Edition
February 2014

Aherm. E? You asked for it! And Mary? You can have it if she doesn't want it. (And Mate—'cause you're still shiny.)

GARDEN PARTY

WILL LAFFERTY thought his aunt Cara's wedding was spec*tacular*!

Held outside, in the brides' backyard in Grass Valley, the event smelled of dusty pine trees and garden flowers. Big granite boulders littered the yard, with irises and snapdragons planted around them to make it look as though they were purely decorative, and the brides (or their faithful helpers) had set chairs and tables to look toward a nice shady spot under a great tree with tiny leaves. There was even a big porch with an extended concrete apron for dancing.

Cara wore a feminine off-white suit, with a cravat and wide-legged slacks. She wore her hair in a Gibson Girl bun, with baby's breath threaded through the graying brown curls that surrounded her face. Her beloved, Nina, wore the full-out wedding frock, narrow around the waist, tiny embroidered daisies complete with yellow-gold centers and pale-green leaves embellishing the frothy tulle of the skirt. Her hair was cut short and colored blonde—with her piquant little face, she looked very Audrey Hepburn except with a dye bottle and a nose stud. Only the fine lines around her eyes revealed that she too was in her early forties.

Kenny cried on Will's shoulder the entire time.

Will just beamed. He'd never seen Aunt Cara so happy.

The ceremony didn't take long—long enough for Will to hold Kenny's hand and watch his mother, the one bridesmaid, wipe away some happy tears herself.

At the reception, Will told Kenny to splash water on his face and gave him eye drops to clear up the red. Afterward, the two of them sat in a corner and picked at a single plate of vegetables and, together, deconstructed the wedding.

"Cara looked amazing," Kenny said dreamily. The bride in question was making the rounds to the tables to make sure everyone was having a good time. Her laughter rang across the yard more times than Will could count. "I have to admit, when I first saw Cara, I didn't think she'd clean up that nice."

"You were so nervous that day," Will said, rolling his eyes. "You thought everybody in the room was a giant Kenny-eating troll!"

Kenny sniffed delicately. "Well, yes. But she's really rocking the suit today. And your mother—she looked thrilled."

Will watched as his mother shooed Cara from one table to the next.

Anne Lafferty looked good today, he thought fondly—she'd actually dressed like the pretty woman he thought she was. Today, she'd worn a white fitted shell and a full skirt with daisies on it. She'd slimmed down a little, so her comfortably middle-aged body was just a little *less* comfortable and more svelte, and she'd actually *dyed* her shoulder-length brownish hair a fashionable red and let a stylist have a go at it. Until after the pictures, actually, it had looked "done," in soft waves around her face. Once the pictures were over, she'd grabbed a scrunchie that looked like a bunch of joined daisies and pulled that mess (her words) back from her face.

"Not as thrilled as the bride," William said warmly, and Kenny rolled his eyes.

"Nina really *is* everything your mom thought she'd be, isn't she?"

William had to laugh. For about a half a minute, Will's mom had thought she'd try to match Will up with Nina—way before anybody had come out of the closet, of course, and only because her son seemed to be terminally lonely.

Well, he had been, William thought fondly, looking at Kenny, who was pretending he wasn't jealous as all hell.

He'd been so lonely, he hadn't been able to see how lonely he really was.

In a swish of satin and tulle, the blonde bride with the Audrey Hepburn face and the tiny diamond nose stud rustled up to their table. With a quirky smile, she sat down at their table and made an exaggerated sigh.

"Whoo! I'm exhausted!" With that, she turned toward the preadolescent girl who had followed her to the table. "Ashley, be a luv and go get your aunt Nina a really big glass of punch, okay?"

The girl had mouse-brown hair and a thin little face. She was wearing a dress much like her aunt Nina's, only more tailored for a little girl's Easter and less for a grown woman's wedding. "Aunt Nina, they only *have* one size glass for the punch."

Nina laughed a little and dimpled. "Then you'll have to get me two, precious. I'm *thirsty!*"

"Okay! I'll be back!" And the girl skipped gaily away.

Nina turned those devastating dimples on William and Kenny, and William had to admit, even though she was about ten years Will's senior, she was a *very* pretty woman. It was a good thing William had met Kenny first, or that gamine face and blinding smile might have made Will forget some very important doubts he'd had about himself—and women in general.

"Okay, boys, so here's my chance. For an entire month, I hear nothing from Anne and Cara but what a *wonderful* boy Will is, and how he and I would make this *stunning* couple, and then suddenly, poof!" She waved her fingers and laughed at the pun. "And then, you know, Cara and I hook up, and by the time we come up for air"—she smirked—"you're a couple. How did that happen?"

Will smiled sunnily at her. Oh, she was wonderful—he'd enjoyed her company pretty much from the moment they'd met. He *loved* people with a sense of humor and who loved a good story. He'd heard *her* story already. The first time he'd met her at his mother's house, Kenny and Will had heard all the details—and they'd been sweet, exactly what he wanted for his beloved aunt Cara who had snuck him sweets and hugs and who had taken him out to her farm since he was very small.

"You don't want to know that story," he said, not wanting to intrude on her perfect day.

"Of course she does!" Kenny said, straightening from his slouch at the table. His dark hair—which sort of artfully tumbled from standing up straight on his head—was perfect, and the tiniest bit of guyliner he'd used that morning made his blue eyes stand out. His face was all hooks—chin, nose, cheekbones—and Will sometimes told him that it was a great face because it had just hooked Will right in, hadn't it? He was wearing a truly shocking turquoise suit jacket with a lime-colored paisley liner displayed at the collar, and a lime tie. His pants were race-car red, and he looked like the thin, artistic swirls of color on a birthday cupcake. William was wearing a basic navy-blue suit, but he'd been following Kenny's bright plumage with his eyes all day. That much color attracted him like a big red plastic flower full of sugary goodness attracted a hummingbird.

"No, she doesn't," Will protested, blushing, and Kenny went from insouciant party observer to center of attention in 0.05 seconds flat.

"Of course she does!" Kenny repeated, sitting up excitedly. "You haven't heard this story? Not at all?"

Will blushed even more. "Kennnneee! My *mother* hasn't even heard this story."

Kenny grinned wickedly and Will covered his face in mortification. "Oh come *on,* Will—you've got to admit, it's a *great* story!"

At that point, Ashley returned with two glasses of punch, and Nina set the cups down and grinned at the two of them. The crowd was starting to dance, and the DJ was playing at just the right tempo and volume—not too loud to talk and fast enough to make dancing fun. "I'll tell you what," she said, clearly enjoying herself. "I'll have Ashley keep us supplied with cake and punch if *you* tell me the story of how you met."

Kenny looked up at the little girl sardonically. "Okay, sweetcheeks, but I've got to tell you—she's going to be run off her little tushie, because a *lot* of this story is *not* suitable for children."

Ashley grinned. "My aunt's a lesbian and my dad's in prison for tax evasion. Try me!"

Nina grimaced. "Yup—she's pretty savvy. I'll just bet you won't shock her."

Kenny shrugged. "How 'bout you go get us some cake for the first part, short person. The rest of it is probably pretty PG."

"Did you want the chocolate or the vanilla parts?" Ashley asked, all attention.

"Chocolate!" Kenny said at the same time Will said, "Vanilla!" and Nina threw herself back into her chair and clapped her hands.

"This is going to be *some* story!" she chimed.

Will patted Kenny's knee. "You've got to start it."

"Yes, yes I do." Kenny nodded. "Okay, Nina, you asked for it. Can you remember the worst breakup you ever had?"

Nina pursed her mouth. "You mean when I told my husband I was a lesbian?"

"Oh, ouch! Yeah, that hurts, but Will and I? We got that story beat."

"Oh *man*. Well, get to it, boys. I've got my niece on retainer, we've got a sugar rush barreling down at us in a tulle dress, and Cara is going to be dancing with her uncle for at least another fifteen minutes. I have *got* to hear this!"

Kenny grinned salaciously, and Will couldn't decide whether to groan or kiss him. Kenny really did love telling this part first.

"Okay," he said. "It all started when I got home early one day to surprise my boyfriend...."

THINGS YOU DON'T WANT BACK

ONE OF the best things about having a grown-up job was that you could take long lunches. No, not all the time, but once every other week or so, you could run errands, or take your mother out, or, in Kenny's case, run home for a quickie.

He usually wasn't quite such a horndog, but he'd *just* gotten the job as a graphic designer at the software firm, which was a huge scary deal. He hadn't been home that much in the past two months—he and Gif had been like ships passing in the night, mostly. Hell, he hadn't even been able to collect Gif's share of the rent, much less actually *have sex* with the man, and the last time they'd gone out to the movies had been....

Well, shit. Kenny couldn't remember.

And after two months of working his ass off and noticing the "long lunch" policy was pretty universal as long as you got your work done, he'd figured, what the hell. He'd worked Saturdays for a month—it was time to get some back. So even though he lived in a sketchy little suburb in Citrus Heights instead of a pricey home in Folsom, which would have been closer to the company, he piloted his electric-blue smart car across the river and up Auburn Folsom Road, past the big cemetery with the fountain, and through the suburban maze that was Citrus Heights.

Oh boy oh boy oh boy oh boy, Kenny was gonna get him some today! God, sex! Remember what sex was like? The taste of a man's skin? The feel of his cock in your hand? Oh *hells* yeah! Kenny had even skipped breakfast and done the extra-special bathing ritual so he could have Gif's cock *everywhere* today. Gif's cock was *amazing*, or at least it had been the last time Kenny had actually *touched* it, or had it in his hand, his mouth, his ass, or any of the parts it felt good as a whole.

And it was perfect! Gif worked the night shift as a nurse in Roseville, and he'd worked the last of his string of four shifts the night before. He'd just be waking up when Kenny got home, and he'd be all slender, blond, soft and sleepy man.

Oh geez. Kenny just wanted to rub his tongue all over that man and *come*.

There was a Mercedes parked in front of the neighbor's house, and Kenny had just enough time to sneer at them a little. In *this* neighborhood? The only saving grace was the prim little church, complete with parochial school and playground, right across the street. Other than that, a Mercedes might or might not get its hubcaps stolen in five minutes or less.

Yeah, Kenny was making good money *now*, and so was Gif, for that matter—but when they'd found the house less than a year ago?

No, not so much.

But that was why the college and why the hard work to find a good job, and why Gif was working all the late shifts at the hospital, right? So they could move somewhere that *didn't* look disapprovingly at all the gay pride bumper stickers Kenny had pasted on the back of the smart car like wallpaper.

But enough with the forethought already! Jesus, Kenny just wanted to get *laid*!

He started undressing pretty much the moment he hit the door. Unbuckled went the thick silver-studded belt, down went the nice black jeans with the decorative white seams, off went the fashionably tight purple paisley shirt.

The bright neon turquoise-and-green boxers?

Those he kept on.

He folded the clothes haphazardly on the couch and tiptoed down the hall, careful of the runner, which tended to bunch when Princess, his magnificently fat white Persian cat, tried to run on it. But Princess was asleep in the spare bedroom, on Kenny's office chair, probably plotting how to open his home laptop so she could sleep on the keyboard. Excellent, Kenny wouldn't have to kick her out of the bedroom to—

"*God, yeah, fuck me harder!*"

Kenny's head snapped back. It had been… well, had it been quiet in the house? He'd been in such a hurry, but that was definitely the sounds of someone….

He threw open the door to the bedroom and froze.

There was Gif, the top of his dreams, hands tied behind his back with one of Kenny's brightest interview ties, ass up, facedown on Kenny's brand-new comforter, taking it up the ass from a perfect stranger.

Who, in turn, was taking it up the ass from Kenny's favorite butt plug/cock ring combination.

The one with the neon-green plug and the gaudy brass cock ring.

In that instant that was all Kenny noticed about the guy—he had Kenny's sex toy jammed up his ass and clamping the base of his johnson. Period, the end. *Kenny's* sex toy. The one Kenny had used *frequently* while Gif watched and beat off.

Oh God. Was there *anything* in the goody drawer untainted by this anonymous stranger's ass?

"God, yes, Oscar!" Gif begged. "Don't stop. Don't stop fucking—"

Oscar (apparently) reached forward and dragged Gif's head up by the hair. "Don't tell me what to do, you little bitch," he snapped and then drove deeper into Gif's ass, punctuating the thrust with a hot little pop on his flank.

Kenny watched with fascinated eyes as a red handprint appeared. He had the absurd thought that maybe he should leave and let them finish, and then Gif, who was lying with his head turned so he could breathe with his face mashed into the mattress, caught a glimpse of him out of the corner of his eye.

His knees went out from under him and he flattened on the bed, struggling against the silk tie, while Oscar swore at him to keep his ass up and fuck like a man.

"No, Oscar, my boyfriend—"

"So, he can join us!"

Gif was a big guy, actually, and when Oscar pulled back, he used the opportunity to roll over and struggle with the tie around his wrist.

"No, asshole, *he's right there!*"

Oscar suddenly stopped fucking. He turned around, and Kenny got the impression of a wide-shouldered Hispanic man with broad cheekbones, big brown eyes, and a wickedly handsome smile.

"Your boyfriend isn't really old?" he asked.

Right then, Kenny felt sorry for him.

And then he remembered to feel sorry for himself.

"You're using my butt plug," Kenny said succinctly. "I'd appreciate it if you took that out of your ass."

Later, Kenny couldn't say who moved first. It was sort of a group effort at chaos, really, but the star of the show was Gif, struggling to pull out of the necktie and then put his pants on all at the same time.

Kenny had an advantage—he'd kept his shorts on.

By the time Gif was even halfway dressed in a pair of old scrubs, Kenny had managed to dump a third load of clothes on his front lawn.

"Oh come on," Gif begged. "Kenny, think about this—we've got a house together—"

"It's in my name," Kenny snapped. "You pay rent, remember? Except you haven't *paid* rent for the last two months, so technically, this isn't a breakup, it's an eviction!"

"Well, it's not like we've had sex anytime in the last two months!" Gif snarled, and Kenny actually stopped his stomp back into the house to glare at him.

"That hasn't been all my fault! I try to wake you up all the time— what, were you too sexed out from Oscar here to even *pretend* to want me?"

Oscar had actually taken the time to dress—in a suit with bright patent leather shoes and a tasteful burgundy tie. They couldn't have used *that* to tie Gif's hands? "Hey," Oscar said, holding up his hands. "Don't look at me! He told me you were impotent with a little tiny dick!"

Kenny had stalked past his car by this time and was sheltered from the school by the side of the garage, which was the only reason he had the courage to do what he did next.

Which was to shove his boxers down, grab his larger-than-average penis, and wave it around before pulling his drawers back up and barreling back inside. Behind him, he heard Oscar saying, "Well, I guess Gifford here lies about *lots* of things, doesn't he?"

By the time Kenny returned with Gif's suitcases—filled with more clothes, toiletries, books, and personal electronics—the Mercedes was gone and Gif was still in his jeans, shoving his crap in the back of his blue Toyota.

"Jesus, Kenny, you just had to throw a hissy fit, didn't you?"

"You were boning another man, Gif. In our bed—"

"In *your* bed!" Gif snapped viciously. "Remember? We kept *your* bed, and *your* table, and *your* chairs—"

"Because you were still sleeping in a twin bed and eating over the sink!" Kenny protested, stung. "Remember *that*? You, two roommates, checking your underwear to make sure they'd been washed because Monty kept borrowing them and putting them back in the drawer?"

Gif's evil smile was all Kenny needed.

"Ugh—God, even *then*?"

"Monty had a nine-inch cock, Kenny. *Nine inches*—do you have any idea what—"

"*Stop!*" Kenny's voice cracked. "Jesus, Gif—why even move in with me? I was talking about forever and we actually *picked out and bought curtains*, and you were just... I mean, you were still partying like a college kid!"

Gif's vicious little smirk faded. "I don't know, Kenny. It was a nice dream, I guess. I mean, when I was *with* you, it was really pretty, but, you know, two months—"

"Yeah," Kenny said, finally remembering to drop the two suitcases on the lawn. "Something else came along. Something shiny."

"Well, it couldn't have been that much of a surprise," Gif said with a self-loathing little shrug, and in that moment, Kenny remembered the night they met, in a club in Sacramento, and how Gif had come prepared with a lubed purple rubber and Kenny had gotten the best bathroom fuck *ever*. But then, Kenny had been dressed in a gold lamé shirt and hipster glasses, with leather pants so tight he'd been halfway erect all night because of the friction.

"Yeah, I guess I was shiny too," Kenny said, thinking about it. "For a whole year and a half, I was pretty damned shiny. Don't go yet. I'll bring out the drapes."

The drapes were done in an impressionist pastel floral pattern that sort of made Kenny gag. Of all the things in the house, he'd be happiest to turn those over to Gifford, but sure enough, by the time he could yank them down off the wall by the sliding glass door to the backyard, he heard Gif's car wheezing out of the driveway. The power steering was bad—Kenny could recognize that squeak from two blocks away.

Kenny was left at the front door of his little blue stucco house, holding an armload of drapes and his pretty dreams for the future, with only one place to put them.

It was a good thing trash was picked up the next day, he thought, shoving them into the barrel on top of the old takeout boxes and—oh God, really?—empty boxes of rubbers. Apparently Oscar— or *someone*—had been in Kenny's house a *lot* when he hadn't been paying attention. Abruptly he remembered the sex toys, which were still on the bed.

Oh, gross.

Back into the house, but this time, he had two plastic grocery bags, one to put over his hand and one to shove stuff in, and he didn't stop at the stuff on the bed, oh no. If Oscar had been using *that* thing, who *knew* what else had been used and just thrown back under the bedside table?

Kenny grabbed *everything*—sanitizing wipes, lubricant, *everything*—and shoved it all into the plastic bag willy-nilly. Giant dildos, cock rings, the penis pump, the flesh jack, the nipple clamp/cock ring combo, the progressive turquoise butt plugs that loosened you up so you *could* use the giant dildos, the bright-green vibrating egg, the double-sided wang—all that shit had to go. It barely fit in the bag—Kenny dropped two different vibrators three times on the way out, but eventually he used both hands, covered by the extra plastic bag, and shoved the whole mess on top of the drapes. The lid of the garbage can was open a little, but Kenny didn't have time to think about that right now. He needed to go strip the bed and wash the sheets.

He was still in his boxers, loading the washing machine, when he heard the hollow thump-and-clatter of a vehicle hitting a trash can, and that was when he knew that the impossible had happened.

His day had just gotten worse.

NINA LOOKED over her shoulder to see that Ashley was still standing patiently in line, waiting for cake.

"Oh my God—so you were *living* with a guy—"

"Gifford Boyle—scumbag extraordinaire. We'd been living there for about a year." Kenny took a sip of the punch Ashley had brought him at the beginning of the story, right when he was talking about the house and before he'd stripped down to his underwear.

Will let out a sound approximating a growl, and Nina looked at him in surprise.

"William, that sounded downright possessive!"

William could feel his face tighten and his eyes narrow and his jaw grind, and only Kenny's pat on his leg kept him from breaking something.

"It's okay, precious," Kenny said, keeping his voice light. "The big bad man is all gone now—no need to go into attack mode anymore."

Nina crossed her legs under her fluffy tulle dress and rested her elbow on her knee and her chin on her hand. "This is the best wedding present *ever*," she said breathlessly. "Keep talking!"

"Does that mean we can take back our gif—" Kenny began excitedly.

"No," Nina cut him off. "Whatever it is, I must have it, to remind me of this story right here."

Will smiled to himself, because Kenny had picked out a lovely art deco fruit bowl from Williams-Sonoma that Kenny himself had coveted. Will had gone in and bought the same glass bowl in a lime green instead of a turquoise-tinted glass the next day—it was waiting at home on the table as a sort of present.

"Good," Kenny sniffed. "I wouldn't have taken it back anyway. Will—hon, the next part of the story is yours."

Will smiled and blushed and bit his lip.

"So yeah, William," Nina began, batting her pretty blue eyes at him. "What were you doing while Kenny here was throwing out sex toys in his boxer shorts?"

Will grimaced. "Me? I was getting fired."

"For *what*?" Nina sounded outraged, which was nice—it meant she thought he was reliable.

"For Harry Potter, really," William said, thinking about it. "See, I was teaching fifth grade at the church school across the street...."

MAGIC

"BUT MR. Lafferty, I don't *want* to read the school story. It's boring."

Will sighed. Yeah, it was a Christian school—the curriculum was Bible oriented and, well, watered-down Bible at that. If Charlton Heston could make Moses seem interesting, you'd think a school in the modern age could. Well, Will knew better, didn't he?

"'Kay, Carter. I understand. But if you read the school story by Monday so I can pass you for progress reports, you can read something from my shelf after that."

Carter was a plain kid, with brown eyes, a sort of square face, and a thick but able brain. Will could completely identify. Will looked at this kid, saw himself, and thought, *Hey—if someone could show this kid a whole new world, maybe he won't go out, get a shitty low-paying job, and marry the first girl who feels sorry for him.*

And then he realized that was probably what was going to happen to *him*, six years of college or not, and got depressed. But that didn't keep him from trying.

And in this case, Carter's face lit up. "Yeah? Because the other kids are talking about the *Star Wars* books—those sound neat!"

Will grinned. "Absolutely. But work first, play later." *Because work is never as much fun as the playing. Ever. It's impossible.* But that was another secret grown-up truth Will kept to himself.

The kid nodded eagerly and turned around to take off, almost running into Miss Maggie, the terrifying principal of the little church school in the run-down neighborhood.

Miss Maggie paused in the doorway and perused Will's room, and Will grinned at her, hoping she'd like what he'd done with the place over the past eight months. Well, sure, it was just a little portable building, like much of the school, but he'd imbued it with book posters and movie posters—age appropriate, of course—and, hopefully, some charm, which would make attending a parochial school somewhat appealing.

Miss Maggie grimaced. She did not, all things considered, look appealed to. "Will, you *are* aware that you teach in a parochial Christian school, aren't you?"

Will tucked his hands in the pockets of his brown corduroys and shuffled his feet. "Nice to see you today, Miss Maggie!" he said, and she shook her head.

"Will, answer the question, please. You do know this is a church school. You're aware it's a rather conservative denomination and this is a private school run through the church, right? We hired you in September, and it's May. Please tell me that set in."

Aw, hell. What had he done now?

"Well, yeah, Miss Maggie," he said, trying to smile. "That's why I get paid the big bucks!"

The formidable woman with the iron-gray hair pulled back in the old-fashioned bun was not amused. She should have been—private schools paid fully three-quarters of what public schools did, and in California (well, in anywhere, really) that first figure wasn't enough to pay the rent.

Which was why Will worked a second job as a web designer in his spare time. His business was picking up—he made almost as much doing that as he did teaching, but *damn*, did he not want to try living on that income at this juncture.

"Will, you know you signed a contract that said that even though you don't attend church here, you had to live your life by the same morality code."

"Uhm, yeah?" Sadly enough, nothing in Will's life had violated anybody's morality code in quite some time. Or by much of a margin, really.

"Then you're aware that all of this"—she indicated with a sweeping gesture—"is a clear violation of your contract?" And effectively she swept away Will's free-reading bookshelf, painfully built up from garage sales, library sales, and Scholastic book donations.

Will gaped at her, sure there was a joke somewhere, but he didn't see it. Miss Maggie's reddened features were sternly lined, and she glared at him from under thick black brows and behind thick black-framed glasses. Her long denim skirt and blue polo shirt might have *seemed* casual, but since women weren't allowed to wear pants in this denomination, Will knew it for the uniform it was.

"They're books," he said weakly, trying a smile. "Good books. The kids love them!"

Miss Maggie shook her head, and for the first time, Will saw some compassion in her uncompromising features. Her flat, grim mouth even relaxed for a moment. "Look—don't take this personally, okay? I know you're a good person—and probably even a good teacher. But you're teaching at a church school. I'm not sure you realize what that means."

Will nodded and spread his arms in a "Hey, look at me!" gesture. "I'm a totally average, normal, Christian-looking dude!" he claimed. He *was*. His entire demeanor had been carefully crafted, from brown corduroy pants to brown-and-cream plaid button-up shirt, with T-shirt underneath in spite of the spring day in the nineties. His plain brown hair was unremarkably cut, swept from a side part across his brow in a style that was probably fifty years old, and his brown oxfords were the same shoes worn by boring teachers who had needed the Dr. Scholl's inserts since time before time.

Miss Maggie grimaced and pinched the bridge of her nose. "Will, we don't ask you to be a member of our church—or even to be a totally average-looking man. But what's *in your head* does not conform to our curriculum. First, there was evolution—"

Will swallowed. "Okay, in my defense, I had no idea that was a religious thing. I thought it was just common sen—yeah. I'm sorry. No dinosaurs again, I swear."

Again, that almost grandmotherly look of compassion as she gestured to the bookshelf. "Will? Harry Potter? Witchcraft. Sorcery. Percy Jackson—that's mythology, the worship of other gods. *The Primrose Path*—that one completely denounces the church's missionary work. Charlie Bone, The Chronicles of Prydain, Robin McKinley—do you have a book on this shelf that clears church guidelines?"

Will had a complete, horrified moment of disconnect. "Those books aren't in the church guidelines?" he asked weakly.

Miss Maggie raised her eyebrows and shook her head like this was common knowledge.

"But... but... this is... you know, twenty-first-century America—this is... just literature! These kids go home and watch reality television and they can't read Harry Potter?"

"We have no control over what the kids read or see when they're at home," Miss Maggie told him. "But when they're *here*, the reading has to meet the requirements of the church. But more than that—Will, you have an *X-Files* poster behind your desk! It says *Trust No One*—we spend twenty minutes in prayer every day asking the kids to trust in God. Has it occurred to you that maybe you're just not cut out for this job?"

Will felt his lower lip quiver. "But... I *love* teaching!" he said frantically, because he did. He loved the dumb fifth-grade jokes the kids told, he loved watching the boys become all elbows and knees and the girls start doing their hair and realizing they were taller, older, and smarter than the boys. He loved watching that whole "aha" thing go down, when they *got* something, and being the one to stretch their little brains out and have them get the next thing, and the next, and the next.

"Maybe so," Miss Maggie said dubiously, "but ask yourself, do you love teaching *here*?"

"But...." Will flailed. "There's nowhere else hiring!" And fuck him if there was! God, in spite of the fact that most fifth graders were crammed into a classroom with thirty-five other kids like raisins in a teeny box, taxpayers and governments seemed to think that was *dandy*, and teachers were coming out of college with nowhere to go. After San Juan—one of the biggest districts in the state—had laid him off, Will had spent two years subbing in some of the worst districts in NorCal, happy that he was at *least* using his credential. Hell, he'd been *thrilled* to land a job at a private school. And since it *was* a private school, he was probably the only person there *with* a credential. In fact, he was probably the only teacher there who *didn't* attend the church, and apparently, that made him expendable. And, well, it wasn't like private schools had a union.

Miss Maggie was nodding as if to confirm his worst fears. "They've taken their STAR tests already, Will. We can have a church elder take over your class for the next month. The one thing we ask our teachers is that church policies be upheld, and it's not a sin on your part, but I really don't think it's something you can do. Please have your stuff cleared out of the classroom before the end of the weekend—but don't come during church services, if you can."

"I can do it right now," Will said numbly.

It took an hour.

An hour, and the past eight months of his life were effectively packed into the back of his car—which was his mother's *old* car, a brown Oldsmobile—and Will was on the phone with the girl who'd been unsubtly hinting they should go out.

"No, Denise," he said wearily. "I don't know why they fired me. Something about Harry Potter—"

"The *movie?*" she snapped, and Will grunted, starting the car so he didn't have to sit in the heat.

"No, Den, the books. I let the kids read them—"

"In a *Christian school?*"

Okay, well, that sealed it. Will was apparently too dumb to teach fifth grade. "They loved them," he said disconsolately. "They loved them—*Star Wars* was okay, how was I to know—" He looked up and saw Miss Maggie staring at the back of his car from the entrance to the church proper, and figured he needed to pull away. It was a simple residential road—he could be off the phone by the time he hit Sunrise Boulevard, where a CHP officer really *might* bust him for cell phone use.

Carefully, he pulled forward while Denise continued to chew him out. "Jesus, Will, how are you going to pay your bills? Remember we were talking about going wine tasting?"

"I don't want to go wine tasting," he told her bluntly, because he'd been trying to get out of it *nicely*, but that was when he still had brain cells for tact. "*You* want to go wine tasting. *I* want to stay home and work on my business!"

"But your business is just a pipe dream—how are we going to *live?*"

"We?" He actually looked at the phone.

And then hit a garbage can in the middle of the street.

"*Fuck!*" he swore from the pit of his stomach.

"*Will!*" Denise shrieked, because he *never* swore.

"Look, I've got to go, okay? I just hit some guy's trash can and I need to pick shit up."

"You said 'shit'!" Denise shrilled, and Will hung up.

No shit he said shit—it was all over the road!

Or, well, something was all over the road.

Will pulled over and parked his car in front of the bright little house right across the street from the school. He'd noticed this house before—*liked* this house, because it seemed well cared for in the middle of this very working-class, run-down neighborhood. He hopped out of the car and regarded the somethings all over the road, dealing with the thing he recognized first. Something that looked like a big flowered curtain, which he gathered in his arms and shoved in the can first. Then he turned to the other somethings.

Wait. What were those?

A plastic bag skittered over his foot in the hot wind that blew across the brown playground of the school, and he bent down to start shoving stuff in it.

Without thinking about it, he closed his hand around a reflective gold-plated phallus with a black plastic dial at the bottom.

"Shiny...."

He stared at it, mesmerized, wondering exactly what it did. Of course he *knew* what it did—he'd been with women before—but this thing... well, there was a flexible ring around it that didn't look like it belonged there. It was sort of stretchy and had another attached loop sort of flopping off the bottom, and for a moment, Will just stood in the middle of the road, holding the big gold-plated phallus and staring at the stretchy thing attached.

"Uhm...."

Will yanked his attention from the glittery thing.

"You, uhm, may not want to touch that."

Will looked up and saw a young man with a face that featured a thin nose, sharp cheekbones, and a pointed chin—and a pair of pretty blue eyes surrounded by black lashes.

They stared at each other, and then Will realized that the young man's paisley boxer shorts were also a pretty blue and green. And that he was standing in the middle of the road surrounded by—well—

"What is this?"

"It's a gold-plated vibrator and a cock ring I wrapped around it because I use them both together."

Will blinked. "But you're not married! We *never* see a woman over here." Because Will had just remembered that he'd seen this young man with his pleasing, pointed face leaving in the morning as he had been arriving. There'd been another man with blond hair that Will hadn't really noticed, but this one... well, even when he wasn't in his boxer shorts, he was something to pay attention to.

The young man's eyes grew round and his eyebrows arched. "No, precious, there *isn't* a woman around here. There used to be a *man* around here, but we broke up."

Will squinted at him in confusion and then looked at the thing in his hands. "But then, what's *this* for?"

The young man just looked at him, blue eyes wide. He didn't even blink. "I'd give you three guesses, precious, but you only have one."

Will's eyes narrowed and his jaw dropped and he looked at the other detritus scattered at his feet. His shoulders jerked and he thought about dropping the thing in his hand, but it was so round... so *cylindrical*, so hard, and he found he was stroking it as he tried to assimilate the scenario.

"But... but... that's *personal*!" he said, and even *Will* couldn't have said what he was referring to—the toys or their intended orifices and staffs. "Why would you throw them away?"

The young man shook his head and the spell was broken. With a sigh, he bent down and looked around, wandering in a circle in his bare feet on the badly paved road. He came up with a box of what looked to be sanitary wipes. He reached in and grabbed a few and then very gently shoved them in the hand not holding the big metal thing (*dildo*? Was *that* what this was?).

"Because, precious, I just caught my boyfriend cheating on me, and I don't know where that thing's been."

Will dropped the dildo like it was made of napalm, and the man thrust another handful of sanitary wipes into his hand before he could start dancing like a fool screaming, "Get it off! Get it off! Get it off!"

He wiped his hand silently instead and then took a cue from the other guy and grabbed a plastic bag. Gingerly, he started using it like a glove to pick up the other toys off the road and throw them away again, on top of the curtains.

"Thanks," the other man said dispiritedly. "You didn't have to do this."

Will forgot what he was picking up for a minute (but they were turquoise and there were three of them and they came in graduated sizes) and looked at his car parked on the side of the road. "I was the dumbshit who knocked over your trash can. It's the least I could do. It was the—"

"Perfect end to the perfect day," they both said synchronously, and then stopped and looked at each other, and then looked at the last of what even Will had to admit was a vast array of unusable sex toys.

"Look," he said, "uhm—"

"Kenny," the young man supplied.

"Kenny? It's Friday, I just lost my job, you just lost your boyfriend and your—" He struggled for a word. "—accoutrements."

Kenny grinned tiredly and nodded for him to continue.

"How about we get this squared away, you go put some pants on, and I'll take you out for a beer?"

Kenny gaped for a minute and then stood up straight and waved his hands. Will had a moment to realize that the shorter man's body was small and wiry, and his stomach was defined, and his lightly hairy chest was rippled too, and he'd never noticed those things about a man before, but that wasn't his focus right now.

"But... but...," Kenny sputtered, "I'm *gay*!"

Will laughed and shook his head. "Yeah, but at least you're not a witch," he said and reached down to gather the rest of the weirdness from the road.

Kenny let him into the house to wash his hands (thank *God*—he didn't want to face what else might have been on that big glittery thing he'd picked up from the trash), and while Kenny went to put on some clothes, Will stood in the kitchen area and looked around. Like the blue stucco exterior, the interior was pleasant, colorful, and unassuming. A white tiled floor needed a light mopping, and the battered standard-issue maple table still had three days' mail and a place mat with crumbs from breakfast.

But it also held a vase with some flowers that were still fresh, and the tweed-covered furniture in the living room looked used but clean. The wide-screen was set back in an entertainment center that had a colorful throw on top, with some abstract sculptures set up on it. A large framed print of José González's *In Our Nature* album cover sat on the wall over the fireplace next to Loreena McKennitt's *Book of Secrets* and Mumford & Sons' *Sigh No More*.

It was a nice, clean space, Will decided, not too cluttered, not too spare. The carpet was a surprisingly bold blue, and there was a bookshelf opposite the television. Will wandered over and looked at some titles, surprised that he had some of the same ones. Actually, he had a lot of them in the trunk of his car.

Harry Potter and Harry Dresden were well represented, as were Simon R. Green, Isaac Asimov, and Robert Heinlein.

"Wow," he murmured, pulling out *Stranger in a Strange Land*, the special edition.

"I haven't read it yet," Kenny said, wandering in from the bedroom. In his arms he had a stack of sheets that looked like they'd just been pulled from the linen closet. "I was waiting to treat myself after work slowed down."

"Want help with that?" Will asked sunnily. He hated doing housework.

Kenny cast a disbelieving look at him and shook his head. "That's okay, precious—I'll do this one on my own."

Will wrinkled his nose, trying to figure out what sexual innuendo he'd missed *now*, when he heard the rapid spritz of the Febreze bottle. About ten seconds later, a cloud of chemical freshness roiled down the hallway, and Will grimaced.

Okay, time line. *Today.* He'd caught his boyfriend cheating, ditched the boyfriend, ditched the sex toys, washed the sheets.

And then some bozo knocked over his trash can.

Will was all caught up now. Okay, good.

Kenny came back out and grabbed his phone, wallet, and car keys from the charging station on the bookshelf, and Will put the book back.

"You can borrow it if you want," Kenny offered to Will's surprise. "I mean, I see your car every day. You work across the street, right?"

Will grimaced. "Not. Anymore."

Kenny blinked. "Ah."

"Yeah."

"Hence, beer."

Will smiled. "You ready for that?"

"You go out drinking much?

Will didn't even have to think about it. "Never," he said promptly. "Not even in college. I lived at home—who wants to go home to your mother shitfaced and puke on her shoes?"

Kenny's laugh was semihysterical. He covered his mouth with his hand and tried to push it back. "Really? Lived with your mother?"

Will shrugged, not particularly ashamed. "Hey, my mom's amazing. After my dad died, she started her own business doing publicity for *other* small businesses. And seriously, it wasn't like I was going to just... *lunge* off the leash, you know? Not in my nature."

Kenny seemed to remember something. His face softened for a moment, and when he looked back at Will, one corner of his mouth curled up. But other than that, he seemed thoughtful. "Nothing wrong with knowing yourself," he said as though he was thinking about it. "Do you *still* live with your mother?"

Will shook his head and thrust his hands in his pockets self-consciously. "I'm sort of a night owl when I don't have work in the morning. Mom's an early bird. We used to have the most fearsome fights when I'd stay up until five and she'd get up at four." He sighed. "And unless I can find another job, we may have those fights again real soon!"

Kenny grimaced in sympathy. "And hence, beer," he said again, and Will smiled again, because at least Kenny knew how to banter.

"Absolutely. Your car or mine?"

"Here, let me make sure Princess has enough food and water, and we'll take yours. I know myself too—I'm going to drink until I puke. You good with that?"

Will grinned. Why wouldn't he be? He could spend more time with this energetic man who liked the same geeky music and the same geeky books Will did. The alcohol? That was just an excuse to talk, right?

"FAMOUS LAST words," Nina said drily. "You notice we're serving punch and not champagne."

"That's probably a good idea." Will's nod had nothing in it but earnest intention, but he didn't miss the way Kenny patted his knee sympathetically. Yeah, turned out beer wasn't one of Will's strengths after all.

STRAIGHT-UP FRIENDS

"BUT... BUT... but I don't understand where it *goes*!"

Kenny laughed at Will outright as he sat at the bar, chin resting in his hands, looking mournfully at the second long draft glass on the table in front of him. Oh, sweet baby boy—Kenny couldn't believe a drink had been his idea.

Kenny knew a basic watering hole on Greenback, one of those places in strip malls that looked too seedy to stay in business but that had enough cars in front of it to *never* go broke. It wasn't a gay bar, but it wasn't a redneck bar either. The interior was dark, windowless, and subdued. People were there to drink someplace not alone, and not to get in anyone's business. Yeah, there was some picking up, and probably some drugs in the bathrooms, but nobody wanted to make trouble.

Will had known enough to ask for house draft but not enough to stop after one, but Kenny hadn't minded. He'd nursed his cosmo and engaged in a whole new kinky and unexplored form of intercourse that he and Gifford had never really gone in for.

Talking.

Will Lafferty could really talk.

Not in an obnoxious way either—in an *interested* way.

"So you're a graphic designer," he'd started as they sat down—because Kenny had given out that much on the drive over in Will's vast sailing ship of a grandma car. "That's awesome. Do you design games? Logos? Do you make cartoons? Because that would be *cool*. Do you ever go to the anime and sci-fi conventions?"

For a moment Kenny considered being overwhelmed, but then he realized that not only did Will speak his language, he apparently lived in Kenny's home country.

"Yes!" Kenny exclaimed excitedly. "See, that's why I went to design school. Not, like, you know, a real BA—like a three-year course in graphics. Anyway, they were all about how to get a job in the real world, and all I wanted to do was draw comics and stuff. But I could never think of a storyline, you know? I have these *great* scenarios for like, three frames, but I could never put them together for an arc, you know?"

"Oh my God, I *do* know, and I'm so jealous. I can *write* the arc— not the detail stuff, but I've got these, like, ten-page short stories, and I have catalogs of world-building details, but I just… it's like if someone could, like, film the story in my head or something, I'd have enough for an entire work, but I don't have any patience for the prose, you know?"

Kenny grinned at him delightedly. "I know! Think we're too spoiled? I mean, I remember teachers complaining about that for the longest time—that we were spoiled for visual details and the words were the hard thing."

William took a long draft of his beer and nodded. "Yeah, well, maybe we should just consider it an emerging art form and get over it. People love it, right? It… I don't know, fills a need. It's *important.*" Will's mood changed suddenly then, and he grew morose and a little hurt. "Just because it's new or fantastical, that doesn't mean it's not important."

Kenny thought about moving the chatter along, changing the subject—or going back to graphic novels, because it was a favorite of his—but he paused. At first glance, the guy picking his trash up off the street had been unremarkable. Tall, stocky, with broad shoulders, Will moved awkwardly, like he was used to minimizing his size but remained fully aware he wasn't graceful. His face was square, and if he'd been any wider for his height his features would have transcended square and broken the boundaries to round. His plain brown hair was longish, swept from a side part just like Jem Finch, and he had a straight, largish nose to match his broad face. His mouth, though… wide, mobile, and inexplicably pink, it looked somehow lush, ripe, virginal, and ready, and Kenny was prompted by his baser instincts to do something noble.

He asked why Will got fired.

Will's face lit up, and Kenny felt bad. He couldn't have listened for why the guy was so distracted he'd crashed into a garbage can?

And then Kenny heard the reason, and felt *really* bad.

"Harry Potter?"

Will nodded. "It was like… man, I know they're supposed to be a church school, but getting fired over Harry Potter felt—"

"Sacrifuckinlegious!" Kenny burst out, and Will smiled at him.

"You understand!" he said, and he sounded so heartfelt, Kenny patted his shoulder. And realized how muscular he really was.

"I do!" Kenny said, squeezing his shoulder, and then his bicep. He moved to Will's pec and thought, *Maybe just a little more conditioning there, but really, not bad*—and then he jerked his hand back. Yeah. Groping the straight guy.

Who didn't seem to have noticed, thank fuck.

"You do understand," Will said, leaning even closer to him and looking very earnest. "See, Denise didn't understand. She screamed at me because now I'm not going to be making any money, but I didn't want to go out with her anyway!"

Single! Kenny's inner voice chimed. *Single guy!* And then his other voice snapped, *Straight guy. Single straight guy.* "Why didn't you want to go out with Denise?" Kenny asked desperately. "Skanky? Mean? Already picking out china?"

And then Will shot him a trusting look from supposedly average brown eyes that were suddenly large, limpid pools of vulnerability right there. "I don't know," he said, sounding really lost. "She just… I don't know. Kissing her was like kissing my mom's cat."

"Furry?" Kenny asked, puzzled.

"No, Mom's got a hairless, so really, it's just, you know. Warm and sort of reptilian at the same time."

"*Ew!*" Kenny exclaimed, looking at him in horror. "Jesus, buddy—did you hook up with a mutant or something?"

Will sighed. "She even *sounded* like Deucalion."

"Your mom named her cat after the lord of hell?"

The sound that vibrated up from Will's chest was positively *filthy*. "Have you ever heard a hairless cat? They *all* sound like the lords of hell! But no—it wasn't just her. *All* girls feel like that to me. I mean, it's why I'm not really excited about dating. I'm poor, I'm geeky, I'm sort of unattractive—it's not like they're going to be trying to teach me what it's all about, you know?"

Kenny had never actually felt his eyes widen before. Ever. But... but... he'd *found one*. Weren't they, like, a myth or something? The famous gay guy who didn't *really know he was gay*? Naw... no. Couldn't possibly exist. Asexual was more likely than a sweet guy like this not knowing he was gay. But, well... he could always check. Kenny set his cosmo down and rested his chin on his palm.

"Well," he said patiently, "have you ever thought you're playing for the wrong team?"

"I *like* playing for the Alliance. What does *WOW* have to do with it?"

Kenny's brain did such a quick track change that his eyes popped as he tried not to let it derail. "Never mind," he said, patting Will's shoulder. "But I like playing for the Alliance too."

"Really?" Will's smile was so winsome, Kenny believed in Santa Claus all over again. "Maybe we can play!"

Kenny sighed. "Yeah, why not? Now that Gif is gone—he thought it was bullshit, you know? But seriously, ten hours a week? What harm is there in that? It's not like I watch sports!"

Will huffed out a sigh. "I don't get football at *all*," he agreed. He finished his first draft and looked at Kenny sympathetically. "So you didn't have any warning?" he asked, and Kenny signaled the bartender for another draft. "Really? I wasn't going to be the one who got drunk!"

Kenny laughed and squeezed his arm again because he couldn't help it. Muscly! "Too late, precious," he said fondly. "No worries. You'll have to sleep on *my* couch, but it's comfy."

"Yeah," Will said with a smile. "I like your house. It's pretty. Mine has, like, a bed in one room and a couch in the other, and everything else is books and a computer desk. But you didn't have any warning?"

And oh snap! They were back on Kenny again. Kenny was annoyed at first, and then he was sort of flattered—Will actually cared.

No blowing off Kenny's sad story for his own—the fate of the guy with the sex toys in the road was actually important to him.

Nice. Will was a genuinely nice guy. Go figure.

"Probably," Kenny said, forced into honesty by those guileless and concerned brown eyes. "I mean, I was taking a long lunch because I knew we needed time to connect, but it was more than that."

Will was sitting at the bar, his shoulders hunched and his hands in his lap. It was almost a hapless loser pose, and Kenny didn't like to see him like that.

"Sit up straight and put your elbows on the bar," he advised, and Will complied without asking. There. Just like that, he looked like a sexy bruiser and not a sci-fi geek. He looked possessive over his beer and desirable, and Kenny got to live the illusion of being out with a big, succulent bear daddy who would take care of Kenny's twink ass and keep him safe forever and ever.

"Okay, I'm sitting all assertive-like," Will said, smiling like he was not fooled for a minute. "Now tell me what you were going to say."

Kenny sighed and slouched over his empty cosmo glass. "Okay, I guess I was going to say that... I mean, he was hot, and he had a job, and the sex was *great*"—Will made a suspicious noise that Kenny conveniently ignored—"but I just... I mean, I *wanted* that house to be real, you know? My parents may be Mr. and Mrs. Boring in Davis, but I sort of wanted that. And I thought I'd at least *started* on my way to that, right? To having a friend for life? A future?"

"Mm." It was an indeterminate sound, but Will was nodding like he got it. "No, I know what you mean. You weren't sure if he was the love of your life, but you at least thought you'd started your life, right?"

Kenny nodded, thinking that he was pretty perceptive for a drunken grade-school teacher. "Exactly!" he said, squeezing Will's bicep again instead of slapping him on the back. God... that arm... just didn't get squishier, did it?

"I'm sorry about that," Will said, sounding genuinely sorry. "That must have really hurt—especially when he was using your private things with a stranger."

Kenny's breath caught and Will downed about a quarter of his beer. "Yeah," he said, looking at Will like he'd suddenly shed his skin and come out on the other side looking like the love child of Tyler Hoechlin, Tyler Posey, *and* Dylan O'Brien. "That's what hurt most, I guess. It was like, if he'd *just* been cheating on me, that would have hurt, but that would have been his problem. He *involved* me in his shitty way of treating people. Made it hurt more."

Will nodded and rubbed a little circle in the center of Kenny's back. "That's a shame. You seem like a great guy—I'm so sorry your heart got broken."

Kenny frowned and probed the sore spot of his breakup with his emotions like you'd probe an aching tooth with your tongue. "Not broken," he said consideringly. "Battered a little, but not broken."

Will's grin was pure sunshine relief. "*Awesome*, because now I can ask some *really* inappropriate questions!"

Oh shit! Retreat! Retreat! Retreat! Retreat! "Oh hell no! Will, I can *not* be your gay sex advisor on this one—"

Will took another gulp of beer and shook his head. "No—no, I mean, I *think* I know what some of that stuff was for, but… but…."

No, no, no, no, no, no. Kenny should have been ready for this the whole time.

"I don't understand where it goes!"

And now they were all caught up.

Kenny sighed and fiddled with his cosmo. "You know the answer to that," he said resignedly, and Will grunted into the last two inches of beer.

"Okay—I do sort of," he admitted. "I mean… okay… assuming it can fit—"

"Bartender—one of each!" Because if he was going to answer this, he was going to need more.

If he was hoping the interruption and a fresh drink was going to make Will let go of his bone (get it? A man with a bone? Yeah, Kenny really was going to have to switch to coffee!), he was sorely disappointed.

"I mean," Will said as soon as their drinks were back, "it looked so *big*!"

Ah, hell. He really *was* going to have to give the ass-fucking-for-straight-guys lecture. If he didn't like Will so much, he'd consider it punishment from the sex gods for throwing his toys away in the first place. He had a dishwasher! He could have set it on sanitize, right? Oh gross, no. Better to talk to Will!

"Well," Kenny said, dropping his voice, "I want you to imagine the biggest thing you've ever pushed *out* of that place, and tell me if they compare."

Will sat up straighter and actually... crap. Kenny did not even want to *think* about the cavalcade of prodigious excrement parading behind his eyes. 'Cause he checked, right? *All* guys checked!

"Okay," Will said after a moment. "I see your point."

Kenny closed his eyes and thanked God they hadn't ordered food. "Well, you know how it feels going out? Well, it feels even *better* going in."

"Oh." Will's eyes turned inward for a moment, and as awkward as the moment was, Kenny had to admit it—Will was taking it like a champ. (Smirk, eye roll, sputter.) "Okay," Will said, seriously thinking about it. "Okay. You're right." He turned to Kenny with a brilliant, beaming smile on his face. "Wow. Okay, now I'm seriously wondering what that would be like!"

Kenny tried not to whimper. Big eyes, wide pink mouth, tasty shoulders, and this sort of sweet, genuine kindness Kenny could not ever remember coming into contact with before. Kenny leaned forward and thought, *Hey! I could be the next virgin killer! I could! Get him another beer, take him home, let him ravish me, then tell him it didn't happen so he could pretend it wasn't* great! His groin swelled and ached, and his hands *tingled* to see what kind of skin Will had under that *really* unflattering white plaid shirt.

Then Will blinked and smiled into Kenny's eyes with an absolute lack of guile, and Kenny let out a huge breath. He looked up and caught the bartender's eyes and said, "Two orders of bacon cheese fries, okay?" His groin gave an unhappy little jerk in his pants, but he told Little Kenny to stand the hell down. This boy was not for them.

The bartender, a wiry, ginger-haired man in his fifties, nodded enthusiastically, and Kenny wondered how much he'd heard.

"I think that's a *very* good idea," he said seriously, and Kenny turned to Will with resignation.

"So let's get some bacon cheese fries, and when I'm feeling steadier, how about I take you to the place that will answer all your questions, okay?"

"Awesome!" Will agreed. "And after that, maybe we can have some ice cream!"

Kenny shrugged. And then ice cream. Why the hell not?

"OH GOD!" Will hid his face behind his hands. "I could not *possibly* have been that naïve!"

Kenny nodded at Nina, shuddering from the memory. "Oh, believe it," he said grimly. He dropped his voice and looked for Ashley, who was *just* getting the cake from the caterer and starting on her way back. "Worst case of blue balls I've had in my *life*!" Will heard him confess.

Will moaned. "I'm sorry. I'm *so* sorry!"

Nina nodded with no trace of levity—only her over-bright eyes revealed that she thought this was as funny as hell. "Look at him," she said, a sweet smile on her face.

Kenny turned around and socked Will in the arm, and Will yelped, rubbing his bicep. "What?" he asked. He hadn't *done* anything!

"You said you two had nothing in common!" Kenny snapped, and Will and Nina looked at each other and shook their heads.

"Baby," Will said seriously, patting Kenny's knee, "the only thing we have in common right now is that we are listening to you."

Kenny sniffed delicately. "Okay. Well, in that case, it's your turn."

Will shrugged, and then he blushed. "Oh God. Do I *have* to...."

"Yes," Kenny said.

Will felt like he was being punished for something and he still had no idea what he'd done wrong.

"Yes, you do!"

Will looked up at Ashley as she neared with the cake. "Thank you, sweetheart," he said earnestly and took the chocolate one and passed it to Kenny. He took the vanilla one for himself and looked longingly across the yard at the ice chest with the water in it, needing it to balance all the sugar.

"Aunt Nina...," Ashley whined, and Nina laughed understandingly.

"Go get him some water, sweetie, and then you can go play, how's that!"

Ashley kissed Nina on the cheek. "I want to dance with Aunt Cara before she gets tired."

"Deal," Nina said.

Ashley skipped away and Nina leaned forward. "Okay, guys. I give. Where'd you go next?"

Will mumbled into his hands, and she flicked his forehead. "Say it out loud," she prompted.

And he did.

WANK OFF AND KEEP IT SECRET

WILL WOKE up on Kenny's couch in his boxer shorts and undershirt, wondering if his mom's evil hairless cat had crapped in his mouth. And then dropped a car on his head.

Then he wondered where he was.

Then he wondered *who* was shaking his arm and trying to talk to him.

"Will? Will—baby, I'm sorry. I know you don't have anywhere to be right now, and it's Saturday, but I left stuff on my desk I've got to finish at work."

"Kenny?" he mumbled. Slowly he sat up, shedding the light blanket he'd been huddled under.

"Here," Kenny said, looking insufferably perky in a pair of bright-red pants and a red-and-white fitted polo. He handed Will two Tylenol and a glass of water. "This will help."

Will took the Tylenol without question. God... his *head*. "So this is what I was missing through college?" he asked philosophically. "All things considered, I think actually doing my homework was the way to go."

Kenny laughed. "Speak for yourself, precious. I'm pretty sure the best times I had in college were the times I've *forgotten*, before I woke up like this."

Will nodded, then gulped some water. "Good for you. Let me know if those come back to you."

He felt a decidedly tender hand tousling his hair. "Look, I've got to go—I just didn't want you to wake up in an empty house. Take your time—"

Will shook his head and set the empty glass on the coffee table. "No—that's nice of you, but I should go home. I've got a deadline for a web client—I need to take that income while I can."

"Web client?"

"It's my other job. You don't think I can afford my tiny apartment and hand-me-down car on what I make as a teacher, do you?"

"Wow. No wonder you have no social life. Well, it's a good thing I woke you up, then—I was going to let you sleep!"

Will sighed and stood, stretching, his entire big body just arcing up toward the ceiling as he yawned and tried to clear his head. "Nope! No rest for the fired. I should probably call my mom too and see if Denise is still talking to me."

Kenny made a sound—Will wasn't sure what kind—and he realized that his stretch had let his boxers drop below the danger line. He pulled them up and blushed, feeling suddenly exposed. To cover his embarrassment for his tummy—and exposing his treasure trail and almost the treasure—he reached for his clothes from the day before, which were folded at the foot of the couch, and tried to think of something, anything, that would let Kenny know he didn't want last night's camaraderie to end. Embarrassment or not, it was almost a compulsion. He *must* see Kenny again.

"So, you want to hang out tonight?" he asked as he was pulling up his pants. Suddenly he felt foolish. "I mean, you probably have other friends. Never—"

"Actually," Kenny said, looking sort of excited, "bring a thumb drive or—better yet, here, give me your phone."

Will fished it out of his pocket and unlocked it. Kenny took it and started entering his information under Will's People, talking while he texted.

"Name—Kenny Scalia. Occupation—Graphic Designer. Relationship—Will's New Bestie."

Will grinned and pulled his shirt on. "Bestie, huh?"

"Absolutely," Kenny said, still texting. "Camera?"

Will showed him how to work it, and Kenny took a selfie, then added that to his profile. "We're besties? Not that I'm arguing or anything." Most of the people in the credential program had been married. They'd all sort of scattered to the four winds as soon as the nongraduation graduation ceremony had occurred.

"Yeah," Kenny said, finishing up and handing the phone back to Will. "Gif and I settled down, and all of my party friends from college sort of kept partying. Besides—we picked up dildos together. I think that establishes a bond."

Will tucked the phone back in his pocket and chuckled. "Okay, bestie, why was I supposed to bring a thumb drive?"

"Oh yeah! What I meant to say was e-mail me your story arcs and character bibles and stuff. I can work up some sketches and some ideas."

"Really?" Oh wow! "That's awesome—you'd do that?"

Kenny nodded, looking excited. "Yeah—I mean, it sounded like a great project, and I was going to be working a little less anyway." He looked around the little house, which was probably starting to seem empty. "And it'll feel productive," he said at last, simply. "It'll give us a chance to… to get normal, to—"

"Get our lives back on track," Will agreed. "Yeah, I hear you." He sighed. "I'm not going to find anything but sub work until August, and even that will run out in the next three weeks."

"Mm…." Kenny sighed, then brightened. "You know, give me a business card. I've got some friends who might give you some website business."

Will pulled up a corner of his mouth. "Business cards are for real professionals. I'm a 'find me on the Internet' kind of guy."

Kenny grunted and pulled out his own phone, which he shoved imperiously in Will's hands. He was close enough for Will to smell his body soap, which was something surprisingly dark and herbal— sandalwood? Whatever it was, it made Will wish he had a change of clothes so he could shower. It smelled *really* good.

"Well," Kenny said impatiently, "fill in your info!"

"Okay, okay!" Will snapped out of his cologne-smelling stupor and started punching his info into Kenny's phone.

"Name: William Charles Lafferty—"

"Wow."

"Very white."

"You're saying."

Will raised an eyebrow at him. "You've seen my stomach. Lizard bellies have better tans."

Kenny started to laugh, and Will punched in the rest of his info and pressed Save. He handed Kenny's phone back and started searching for his shoes. "By the doorway," Kenny supplied. "Your keys are hanging on the little peg." He checked his own pockets with a jingle and suddenly seemed in an all-fired hurry to get out of there. "There's a clean toothbrush by the sink, and I *really* need to run. Don't forget to lock up when you're done." He took a few steps toward the door, opened it, and said, "The package on your shoes is yours. In case you forgot."

And then he disappeared, closing the door a little harder than Will expected.

Package?

Will made use of the toothbrush and splashed a little water on his face. This was the guest bathroom, and he liked it. White tile, frost-green walls, little seashells. The hand soap smelled like spring rain. He was tempted to venture into Kenny's inner sanctum just so he could smell whatever it was Kenny had been wearing on his skin, because that smell... it sort of surrounded Will, even through the hangover. It was sweet, earthy, exotic—it had been all Will could do not to hold Kenny still, stick his nose into the hollow of Kenny's neck, and just breathe deep to see if it was even better when warmed by Kenny's body heat.

He shivered, set his toothbrush down in the little holder, and rinsed his mouth, feeling better. That would be sort of a violation, he thought firmly, but that didn't mean he didn't want to see Kenny's bedroom. Just... well... to wonder where all those things in the road had gone. And to imagine how they got there.

He shook his head and winced. It was just, well, he didn't remember much after they'd left the bar. They'd gone driving somewhere, and Will had kept talking, and Kenny had kept talking, and the things they'd talked about—well, Will couldn't remember. But he did remember what he'd *thought* about when they'd been talking, and what he'd *thought* about was Kenny, naked, with that stretchy rubber thing around his cock and balls and the glittery thing up his ass.

That sounded simple, and *really* nasty, but the picture in his head? Kenny, his pointed face lax with happiness, his quirky grin softened and sly, and his trim little body stretched out, wanton, naked....

Thinking about it now was making Will tingle with embarrassment.

Right? That *was* embarrassment, wasn't it?

Did embarrassment give you a semi?

Or full-on wood?

Because right now, leaning against Kenny's counter, he was fully, painfully erect, for maybe the first time in months.

He backed away and tried to think about something else— *anything* else. Losing his job, his mother's cat, Denise—oh, there you go. Limp as a politician's moral code.

Will took a step back from the counter and looked at himself in the mirror, wondering why his image didn't change. Same dorky hair, same fat, pink mouth, same big nose. Shouldn't he look different? Look smarter? Skinnier? More hip? Kenny looked hip—cute and perky and hip. Didn't that come with the....

Will shied away from the thought and ran away from the mirror as though it would be that easy to run away from his thoughts.

His shoes were in the hallway, right under the small tiger-striped boutique bag with a short note on a series of green Post-its.

> *If the interest was just the beer, feel free to throw this away and forget it ever happened. If not, I'll field any questions—Kenny*

Will looked inside the bag, wary of the high-gloss crinkle.

And almost died.

THE BAG sat next to him in the car, and by the time he'd made it through Saturday morning traffic, he could swear it was talking to him.

(*Holy crap!* It was wall-to-wall old people. Did *any* of them drive over the speed limit?)

He wasn't sure what to do to shut the bag up.

Heya, remember that big phallic thing? I'm its oddly shaped little brother. And I've got a book! Sure, it's billed *as porn, but it's got* instructions*!*

Instructions with both male and female models.

William stopped at the first McDonald's he came to and ordered a large Dr Pepper and an Egg McMuffin. He'd finished them both by the time he got to his tiny Carmichael apartment, and only the thought of the twelve-pack of Dr Pepper he stocked in his refrigerator kept him from collapsing and weeping before he got through the doorway.

He needed a shower.

And that entire half case of soda.

And some quiet time with that book and that little toy and the little bottle of lubricant.

And *then* he'd look himself in the mirror and figure out what he saw.

He visited the potty for a long time before the shower. When he got out, he wrapped a towel around his waist and grabbed a soda from the tiny fridge in the tinier kitchenette, then downed it in three gulps. The apartment wasn't very big—the kitchen/dinette nook was about one step across, and the couch was three steps from that. The living/dining room was taken up with the computer table, several towers, various laptops, shelves of books, CDs, DVDs, textbooks, and action figures. Everything was shelved neatly and even organized in its own way, but it was, well, *everything.* There were so many shelves, there wasn't any room for posters, and the couch and the small television were like islands of civilization in a sea of nerd-dom.

But, well, it sure was private.

In fact, his biggest worry in terms of privacy was that the sliding glass door to the patio was on the other end of the apartment from the bedroom, but he'd already pulled the heavy drapes.

He heard his phone buzz, and he pulled it out of his pants and plugged it into the charger after setting it on silent. It was his mom. His mom could wait. There were also six messages from Denise, and he had the feeling he had something *really* important to do before he took those calls.

He was tingling all over his body, and just the *thought* of opening that little tiger-striped bag ramped that tingling up higher.

Kiss and Tell, he read from the side of the bag. Vaguely he remembered the place, a little marital aids store on the corner of Fair Oaks and Winding Way, with bright neon signs against the darkness. He remembered sitting in the front seat when Kenny had stopped the car, and when he'd come to, Kenny was getting back *in* the car, so he must have bought this then.

Jesus, what had Will said?

Apparently more about stuff that went in his bottom, he thought practically, brazening out the blush. His hands were sweating and he was practically *shaking* with urgency as he pulled out the contents of the bag.

Will lay on the bed, propping himself up with his arms, and the towel fell open at the back. Well, he thought, spreading his legs a little in the air and feeling decidedly naughty, nobody was here. Nobody could look inside his bedroom—*or* his brain—and this moment here? This was just for him. Via a very nice man who'd had a very bad day.

With that, he grabbed the book from the bag and opened it up to page one.

Oral and Penetrative Sex—The Illustrated Guide.

The title alone made him hard, and he really hadn't even looked at any pictures.

It was a coed book—women and men, in all combinations, demonstrating pretty much every technique under the sun. It must have cost a *fortune*, but… well, damn.

Will had never really *looked* at erotica—in fact, had never considered himself particularly sexual at all. He was very conscious of the fact that he was a big guy, sort of doofy—and, if his recent job situation was anything to gauge by, a *very* poor judge of any social situation.

Who really wanted to get with that?

Once he'd made that realization in middle school, he figured he had two choices. The first was to pine away for some sort of idealized woman he'd never get. The second was simply to enjoy the life he had.

He'd had a couple of relationships in college, but somehow it just really didn't seem worth the effort. There was dating, and even the women who spoke nerd also seemed to want him to speak romance—he couldn't do that. He'd *tried*—"Gee, I had a really nice time. Your lips are perfectly plump, like Liv Tyler's in *Return of the King*—that sort of turns me on!"—but that mostly got him a little smack in the arm and an "Oh Will!" and then, usually, sort of a sad pity fuck. If he heard the words "It happens to everybody!" one more time, he was pretty sure his penis would turn in a resignation card and the only action it would ever see would be his usual trips to the bathroom.

But as he turned the pages of the book, he realized his penis had stopped signing papers and was back in the game.

He turned one page, and there was a lush, happy young woman showing lavish attention to a healthy-sized cock. He felt a decided throb down south, and he shuddered and ground into the towel a little. Okay, yes. *Yes*, that did something to him! He turned to the next page, where two women were tonguing each other's clits.

And his penis started pulling paperwork out of the desk again.

Wait! Wait! Dammit, this thing has some more men in it somewhere—here we go!

A man and a woman together. She was on her back, holding up her knees and spreading herself as wide as possible for deep penetrative sex. The man—thickly muscled chest, tightly muscled ass, a cock that stuck out of his body like a staff of justice—was plowing that field, and hello! Penis alert! We are *fully* engaged! *Completely* interested! Sex alert, sex alert, sex alert! *What else can you look at? Something's finally happening here!*

Will turned the page, and there, in full-color, glossy, two men, beautiful, glistening, muscular men, curled up side by side, sucking each other's cocks to the back of their throats.

The next page featured a close-up of the bottom guy holding a gigantic cock in his hand and closing his eyes against the white spatter of come across his face.

"*Gungh—*"

Will's hips pistoned against the towel and all careful plans evaporated. He shoved his hand under his stomach, grabbed his cock and squeezed, and then convulsed, eyes closed, knees coming up and flopping him to his side, as his body tried to make up for a twenty-eight-year backup of orgasms in one go.

He lay there gasping for a few moments and then closed his eyes and let every feeling, every emotion, plummet back into his body.

He started shaking, but not in fear, or disgust, or denial, or any of the things he might have expected if he ever thought about it.

No. He was shaking in pure, undiluted, unadulterated, untainted *joy*.

"Sex," he murmured. "God, *that's sex!*"

His hand was still wrapped around his cock as he milked the last of his orgasm unconsciously, and now he closed his eyes and allowed a cavalcade of every beautiful man, every actor, every movie star, every sci-fi/fantasy hero, he had ever admired to parade naked behind his eyes.

He started with most of the cast of *The Lord of the Rings*, by height, starting with the shortest.

His cock was partially erect by the time he got to Pippin.

By the time he got to Legolas, he was hard again.

When Aragorn came striding through his brain wearing crotchless leather chaps, he rolled over and looked at the picture book again. Oh yeah. That's it. Will and Aragorn locked in that merciless sixty-nine and Will's face covered in come.

Booya!

TWO HOURS later he changed his sheets and took another shower. He thought about wanking off in the shower, but by then his penis was sort of drooping and raw and saying things like, *For God's sake, give it a break, buddy. I'll keep working if you keep feeding me!*

He felt shaky and spacey and light-headed—

And very, very happy.

THE FIRST thing he did when his house was back to normal was call his mother.

"William, are you all right? Denise has been calling here every hour to see if you've come by."

"How did Denise get your number?" he asked hazily.

"I think she stole it off your phone—she kept saying, 'But don't tell Will I called.' What's the deal with you two? Last time we talked, you weren't dating her."

"I'm not," Will said, focusing on this, at the least. "I'm gay."

There was a pause, and he realized what he had just said. To his *mother*.

"And you're telling me this now? Over the phone?"

"Well, it came up in conversation," he defended himself. "You don't sound surprised."

His mom sighed, and he could imagine her, graying brown hair pulled back into a scrunchie, sleeveless white shirt tucked primly into neutral-colored safari shorts, soft body neither disguised nor enhanced. She had a square face too, and a sort of sweet, womanly jaw and mouth. Will had no idea why she hadn't remarried after his father passed away. Will had been in college at the time, and his mom had grieved and then recovered. Although she wasn't terribly beautiful, she looked *approachable*, and when Will had been dating in school, that was all he'd ever wanted from a girl.

Apparently *approachable* didn't mean stupid.

"Will, my darling, my angel, the light of my life—I'm actually relieved you're gay. You really weren't all that excited about women, and I don't like to think about you lonely."

Aw. Will's mommy loved him. Even big boys needed to know that. He smiled a little and picked the freshly opened can of Dr Pepper up off the end table for a healthy swallow.

"I'll be fine," he said. "I—you're not even a *little* bit shocked?"

"No," she said firmly.

"I don't even know how our family feels about this," he told her, wondering about her parents and his father's parents and—

"Don't tell them," she said, her voice dropping into grim territory. "Nobody but you and me needs to know."

"Oh." Well, it wasn't like he talked with his grandparents much anyway.

"How long have you known?" his mom asked curiously, and he smiled and looked at the clock.

"About three hours now," he said dreamily. "Best three hours of my life."

Was it possible to hear silent laughter?

"Well, then," his mother said, her voice choked, "you obviously still have things to do!"

"Well, no, I'm sort of done now—"

"I gotta go, sweetheart!" She hung up before he even had time to tell her about the job.

That was okay. His next phone call to Denise didn't go nearly as well.

"I'm sorry I didn't call you back," he said once she picked up. "I knocked over a guy's garbage can, and then he took me out for a beer."

"Why'd he do that? Was he trying to sue you?" Denise and both her parents were civil attorneys—it was a natural place for her mind to go.

"No—we were commiserating. He'd lost his boyfriend, I lost my job—you know, making each other feel better?"

"You went out with a gay man?"

Will sighed, thinking about Kenny's pointy face and his lean, fit body and the sort of soulful way he'd looked Will in the eyes a couple of times the night before.

"It wasn't a date," he said, disappointed. "But maybe, after we get to know each other—"

"Will—*we're* going out! You're not gay." She said it like it was a fact, but really, neither thing was true. He pictured her power walking through her upscale neighborhood by the American River, wearing a jogging suit and trainers that cost a week's worth of his salary. It was Saturday—she'd be taking the five-mile route before she went back into the office. Her brown hair would be pulled back severely from her face, and she would have a sun hat on at a ruthless ninety-degree angle to keep her nose from getting any more freckles. The freckles had fooled him, at first. They'd met while waiting for their cars to be serviced, and he'd thought she looked approachable. As it turned out, she just had a lifelong abusive relationship with the sun.

"We're not really going out," he apologized, remembering the tepid kisses that had been more like pecks on the cheek that had landed wrong. "My bad—you're a pretty girl and I kept telling myself it should happen. Now we both know why it shouldn't." God, was he being an asshole? He never knew with Denise. She said she appreciated directness, but he *was* straightforward about his life circumstance, and she'd spent the last four months telling him how to change.

"You're *gay!*" she shrilled, and he pulled the phone away from his ear. "How in the hell do you know you're gay?"

He smiled a little to himself. It was sort of private information, but he figured he owed her a little after the last four months. "Because when I look at pictures of naked men, my penis goes off like a roman candle," he said frankly, and that was when she hung up.

It was an embarrassing conversation anyway. Will was sitting there, looking at his phone in total befuddlement, when he saw the e-mail icon go up by one.

He opened his phone and there was Kenny's e-mail, asking him to send his files on the planet of Calandra, and suddenly the day was much less confusing.

He had a goal and a way to achieve it.

Oh—and a graphic novel to produce too.

"OH MY God!" Nina held her hand very determinedly over her mouth. "*That's* how you found out?"

"How who found out what?"

Cara was coming off the dance floor, sweaty and red-faced and supremely happy. Nina ignored the sweat and stood up to move into her arms and kiss her soundly.

"That's how Will found out he was gay," she said, and Cara looked around her wife's head to wink at Will.

"I'm afraid young William didn't tell me this story," she said, grinning. "Do I want to hear?"

"Nothing to tell, Aunt Cara," William said—partly because she *had* already heard it before, just not in context. You didn't get embarrassed around Aunt Cara. This was his mom's friend, who used to sneak him maple candies when his mom wasn't looking—wholly organic, of course. "Would you like me to get you a water?"

"Sure," Cara said, plopping down and stealing the rest of Will's. "Thanks! Now tell me the story!"

"Well, that was only a short part of it," Nina said. "It was mostly lots of porn—"

"And a date with *me*!" Kenny protested.

Will grinned at him and kissed his knuckles. Kenny had never admitted it was a date before. "Of course," he said. He looked up at Cara and said, "So, how did you know?" He'd been dying to ask, and to his relief, Cara just shrugged.

"It was the damnedest thing. One minute I was boxing tomato plants, and the next minute she was kissing my neck!"

Nina's earthy growl took them all by surprise. "I'd been planning it for weeks. If I'd known that was all it took, I would have moved a *lot* earlier."

Will and Kenny laughed, and Nina resumed her seat, only this time, she was holding her wife's hand.

"Okay—so now we know Will is gay. Tell us the rest!"

Kenny sat up, probably because it was his turn to take over the thread. Will let him. He was curious to see what Kenny would say about this part; to maybe the whole rest of the world, it was really very boring.

To the two of *them*, of course, it was like the universe realigned in assonance.

COFFEE LACED WITH CRACK

"THIS IS good," Kenny said, looking at Will's character bible. Will might not have felt comfortable with prose, but he had a great way of sketching a thumbnail character. "Ernie, species, hominid, furry, *not cute*—sort of like a teddy bear with DNA carved by MC Escher." Kenny looked up from his spot on the couch and grinned at Will. "I can draw this."

Will blinked. "Yeah? He's sort of a layered character—I mean I know he's only a secondary—"

"No, no," Kenny said, opening up his laptop and booting up. He pulled his tablet and stylus out of the pocket in his lime-green case and hooked them up with a cable. "Here…." Oh geez, it always seemed to take forever for the tablet to connect. Okay. Here. His brain was whirling, and he took the stylus to the pad and started working. "Now this is just a minimal thing—I don't know what style you prefer, more pencil lines or bigger, thicker ink lines. I like the finer lines, but some people find that cluttered—"

"No," Will said definitively. "I like the detail you have there. Maybe some heavier lines around the eyes—make them narrow, not all big and round."

"Oooh, yeah," Kenny said, liking that. "No woodland forest creature eyes for this guy, he's gonna fuck you up!"

"Or fuck you," Will said, grimacing.

Kenny looked at the bear and laughed. "Oopsie! Maybe not so much penis in a naked creature." He giggled, feeling completely dorky, and snuck a look at Will.

Who was giggling like a fifth-grader too.

"Oh my God!" Will said, clapping his hand over his mouth. "I hadn't even *gotten* to their mating rituals!"

Kenny's shoulders were shaking, but he still managed to eliminate the stray line and fill it in with sexless fur. "Well, since we want to market to young adults too, let's stick with asexual reproduction," he said firmly, and Will nodded.

"Yeah. That would be best. God knows kids don't have *any* idea what sex is when they're thirteen."

Kenny snorted indelicately. "Then they are looking at entirely the wrong books," he said frankly. "My fist and I were best friends by the time I was thirteen. My mother made me start washing my own sheets—she didn't say why, but trust me, we both knew."

"Yeah?" Will asked curiously, and Kenny snuck a look at him before moving his first sketch aside and starting on one of the two main characters. He hadn't said a word about the little bag Kenny had left on Saturday, not one little word. Kenny figured that maybe it hadn't been up his alley, and he would have felt a little disappointed, but he was having too much fun.

Will had texted him at work that afternoon with an offer of takeout and some character bibles, and, well, hell.

Kenny loved his house—he loved the colors he'd painted the walls (terra-cotta and sky blue), and he loved the wood panel flooring he'd put down without Gif's help, and he loved the new drapes he'd picked out on his way home from work Saturday (green and blue paisley), and he loved his psychotic longhair cat.

What he did *not* love was the prospect of sitting in that house and thinking of all the things that Gif and he would *not* be doing if they hadn't broken up. They wouldn't be watching television, because Gif didn't like sci-fi or crime fic or humor or basically anything with a plot. They wouldn't be listening to music because Gif *only* liked club music, and Kenny liked it *only* when they were going to a club. They wouldn't be going to a club because Gif never had any money to pay for the cover or the drinks, and Kenny was too worried about making the mortgage, even though his job was panning out.

And they wouldn't be taking a walk in the park because Gif thought that was stupid.

So sitting here with this plain, pleasant man, drawing pictures of his dreams—that was a definite improvement.

"What was the sigh for?" Will said, breaking into his thoughts, and Kenny grimaced.

"Sorry. Just... you know...."

Will's look was infinitely compassionate. "You're missing the guy you kicked out three days ago, and I'm not him."

"Well, you're probably better," Kenny said practically. "You're more interesting and you brought food, so I don't think you're a freeloader, but, well, yeah. I keep wondering where I went wrong with Gif."

Will patted his shoulder awkwardly. "Did you see what I brought with the Thai food?" he asked kindly. "I put it in the refrigerator!"

Kenny smiled. "Beer?" Will had reasoned out the trick to good beer—obscure labels. This one had a kangaroo on a bicycle—Kenny figured it could be a one-of-a-kind six-pack in his fridge.

Will nodded and got heavily to his feet. "Glass or bottle? I'll get it if you like—keep working! I like your stuff!"

Kenny grinned and allowed himself to preen. Praise a skill he was proud of—so sue him! It didn't matter that Will was a little plain—square face, square shoulders, meaty thighs—he just sort of radiated this goodwill, like warm peach cobbler. You never got tired of eating warm peach cobbler and ice cream, and so far this evening, Kenny wasn't getting tired of Will.

"I've got chilled glasses in the freezer," he said. "Go ahead and pour us each a glass!"

Kenny lost himself in another sketch, this one of a tiny pet-like alien that rolled on retractable spikes like a sea urchin. This one was *supposed* to be cute, and a little bit deadly, so that, too, was a challenge. By the time Will came back, Kenny had drawn the large, expressive eyes, choosing stylistics over anatomical function and making them hover somewhere around the body amorphously.

Will set the chilled beer mug down with the bottle next to it and then sat down himself with a glass of ice water.

"You're not having beer?" Kenny asked plaintively, and Will shook his head.

"I'm a lightweight," he apologized. "You've seen that. And I brought clothes for the morning, but I may still drive home tonight—

the beer was for you. You've been really nice to put up with me when I'm sure it's the last thing you want to do."

Kenny kicked back a long draft of beer, set the mug down, and filled it from the rest of the bottle. "Good shit!" he praised before taking another sip. And then he addressed the implicit question.

"I'm doing okay," he said carefully. "I mean, I know you saw me at a really, uhm, delicate time, but honestly—I was sitting here, drawing your guys, and thinking of all the reasons I was glad Gif was *not* here." Oh God. For one thing, even if Kenny had known Will *before* the breakup, Gif would not have been kind. Gif was *great* at making snarky, bitchy comments about people who didn't measure up to his standard of beauty or intelligence, and Kenny could hear the litany now. *Jesus, Kenny—this guy's built like a refrigerator. Are you really gonna feed him takeout? Oh my God! Look at his nose—he's like a Roman general without an army! I don't care what he* writes *about, he moves like he's on Thorazine—I bet he's that much fun to hang out with too.* Ruthlessly, Kenny shut down his inner Gif, because seriously? This guy had just brought him fine beer and a fun distraction. If Kenny couldn't defend himself from Gif's infidelity, the least he could do was defend *Will* from Gif's nasty lingering aftertaste.

"Not much company?" Will asked, and he sounded overcasual. Kenny looked up and saw nothing but guileless goodwill.

"Yeah—actually, it was just hitting me what a nozzle the guy was. I mean, it was probably heading for a breakup anyway, right?" Was it? What did it take for Kenny to break up with a guy?

"Well, besides the cheating, what was he like?" Will asked, settling back with his laptop. He tapped desultorily, and Kenny wondered if he was creating a new character or a new arc or adding to what he already had. He was almost afraid to ask—he liked the plot arc for the first two novels so very much, he didn't even want to *see* what else Will could do.

"Well, he's a nurse," Kenny said, because wasn't that the first thing you thought of when you thought of someone?

"Well, that's a nice profession," Will said encouragingly, but Kenny wrinkled his nose.

"There are a lot of serial killers out there who posed as nurses," he told Will, trying to be practical. "I mean, he became a nurse because of the money, and then, in his club days, because of access to poppers, and after twenty-eight days in rehab—paid for by yours truly—I guess he stayed for the cock. I mean... I just don't know when this relationship went from sex all the time to 'he's a giant barnacle on my ass.'"

Will spit his ice water out at the word "cock." Kenny looked at him sputtering and wiping his mouth and trying to regain his composure, and then looked at his beer.

His glass was empty.

"Oh God," he muttered. "I'm sorry—you probably didn't even want to know anything about my—"

"No!" Will stood up and grabbed Kenny's glass, waiting on him in his own home. "No, it's okay. You complain all you want. That's what you do with a breakup, right?" While he was speaking, Kenny heard him in the kitchen, dropping the bottle in the recycle bin, rinsing out his beer glass, drying it off, and then, surprisingly, filling it up again.

"Yeah? I don't hear you complaining about whatserface." Kenny knew what her face was, but given that Will couldn't even hear the word *cock* without choking, he still had sort of a forlorn hope that maybe this plain straight boy wasn't so damned straight.

"Yeah, well, whatserface was never in the picture," Will said, coming back with the beer. He set it down in front of Kenny and kept his refreshed ice water on its own little denim coaster. (Kenny had cut them out of an old pair of Gif's jeans when he'd been in rehab, and for a moment he contemplated throwing them away. But he'd never *told* Gif where the jeans had gone, and had taken a deep, bitter, perverse pleasure in hearing Gif wander the house once a month going, "Kenny, have you seen my favorite jeans?" Yeah. That right there should have been a sign.)

"Why not?" Kenny asked, taking another obscenely large swallow of this *excellent* beer. Apparently kangaroos on bicycles could really hop! Get it? Hop? Cause beer was "hoppy"... oh God. He was giggling to himself. *C'mon, Will, talk, and urge me out of drunken euphoria.*

"I wasn't really attracted to her," Will said baldly, looking at Kenny with sort of a challenge in his eyes, but Kenny... whoo! Kenny was giggling into the dregs of his second beer.

"What's the alcohol content in this shit again?" Kenny asked, looking around for another bottle.

Will's eyes got really big and he checked the bottle.

"Oh for fuck's sake," Will muttered, and Kenny was just aware enough to pay a little bit of attention.

"What?"

"This is like, 17 percent alcohol. Jesus, it might as well be vodka by the twelve-ounce bottle!"

Kenny started giggling again. "I'm *drunk*? Off of two beers?"

Will stood up again and started gathering stuff. "Would you like a third? I'll bring you some crackers and a glass of ice water too."

Kenny remembered to hit Save on his tablet and put it away with his computer, but he didn't get up to put it in the corner with his briefcase when he was done. He was afraid he wasn't going to make it to the door.

"Jesus," he said, confused. "I'm plastered. That was *not* my plan tonight!"

Will was back, like the world's best waiter, with another beer, sans glass, a big glass of ice water and some crackers.

"Yeah, well, I'm sorry. Last time I buy a microbrew to show off."

Aw. That was sweet. Kenny grabbed the ice water and shoved himself to the back of the couch. "You were showing off for me?" he asked. Wow, after two beers, Will's overly square face sort of softened in the corners, and Kenny really noticed his eyes. You know, considering all the times Kenny had been drunk and banged strangers who'd looked *worse* than Will, maybe he wasn't bad-looking after all. Maybe he was *great*-looking; Kenny just had to talk to him sober to see it.

"Yeah," Will said, and Kenny was just drunk enough not to trust that smile. Was it shy? Was it condescending? Was it just friendly? Will seemed to be the sort of up-front guy who would just smile like that, friendly-like.

Which was too bad, because Kenny was sort of hoping it was shy. Shy meant… well…. "Why weren't you attracted to whatserface?" Kenny asked, hoping he sounded sincere.

"She wasn't my type," Will said, pushing himself to the other corner of the couch to mirror Kenny.

"What *is* your type?" Kenny asked, happy, mellow, settling down for a long talk.

"I'm just figuring that out. What's yours?"

Kenny sighed. Well, that was, uhm, vague. "So far, it's slutty and unfaithful."

"That's too bad."

Kenny looked up to see those plain brown eyes looking at him sincerely, and he had a thought to find out some more about this guy. "How come you're not out with your own friends?" he asked.

Will managed a shrug when he couldn't move his shoulders. "How come you're not out with yours?"

Kenny thought about his office, and the people there who sort of moved independently of one another. And about his school friends who were still partying when Kenny had apparently really wanted to settle down.

"I'm between peer groups," he said with dignity. "What about you?"

Will sighed and pulled up his knees. He still dominated the couch, but it was precious of him to think he could crouch there like a little kid. "Well, obviously I didn't have any peers in my old job," he said, and Kenny laughed.

"Obviously." He'd watched the people from that church come and go—the women never wore pants and never cut their hair, and he and Gif had spent the first six months living there expecting the neighborhood association or whatever to politely ask them to leave. That had never happened, and he realized that fundamental didn't necessarily mean unkind—but it certainly didn't mesh well with the sort of educated geekiness Will exuded either.

"And the people in the teaching credential program all had… I don't know. Lives. Grown-up stuff. Families and stuff. It was like, we all graduated and scattered. Which, by the way, is sort of what happens after work too. Even in the bigger schools. We all fought the battle with the kids and then… went home. It was sort of anticlimactic."

Kenny nodded, suddenly feeling the gravitas. "Yeah. That's hard. You want to celebrate with your fellow warriors."

Will nodded. "Right? And we didn't. So there I was, big geeky Will going home to my shitty little apartment, and then I got laid off, and then I subbed, which makes you *no* friends at all, and then I got another job, and… well, you saw how that ended." He sighed.

"Well, what about the website business? How's that going?"

Will shrugged. "You've seen what I do for promotion—"

"Yeah. Jack and shit. C'mon, open your laptop back up. Show me what you can do!"

Well, what he could do was pretty damned impressive. Eye-catching, user-friendly—and he didn't use any of the ready-made templates, so the businesses all looked original.

Kenny hunched over the laptop on the coffee table and very carefully pushed all beverages back from it. "What the…? Pest control?"

Will beamed. "Yeah—do you like the little mice and cockroaches running away?"

Kenny looked at the animated GIFs and had to admit, "Yeah, they do add visual interest. And—organic gardening?"

"Yeah—that's my aunt Cara's business. I mean, she's not really my aunt, but she's my mom's friend—"

"Yeah, yeah—I know how that goes. I had a 'cousin' who used to beat the crap out of me through school. He's like my favorite relative now." Kenny balanced his ice water and made the little air quotes, and Will smiled in understanding.

"Yeah—anyway, she like, mortgaged her entire life to build this little farm and start a business, so I did her website for free."

Kenny looked at it—the pictures were clear and the prose was crisp and unmistakably Will's. "Yeah, this one was designed with love," he said gently, and the waves of joy emanating from Will's big body almost stopped his breath. Wow. A little bit of praise, a little bit of good feeling—this guy was a force to be reckoned with.

"Yeah. Aunt Cara's something else. She's one of those women who just... like, when I was telling her I wanted to get my teaching credential, she was like, 'They'll chew you up and spit you out—and then you'll conquer them like a champion. It'll be fucking glorious. I want a ticket to that show!'"

"Did they?" Kenny asked, suddenly captivated. "I used to be *horrible* to my teachers."

"Well, yeah!" Will nodded. "I mean, I'm a walking fifth-grade joke, right? I knew that going in. But it was worth it. Once they knew me, most of the kids jumped right on board. Sometimes you just need a someone to tell you you're doing a good job, even if it's a big goofy someone who tends to sit in gum."

"They put gum on your chair?"

Will sighed. "I went through a lot of cords in my first year, yeah."

Kenny felt an absurd little wound. "You knew? You knew it would be hard before you did it?"

"Oh yeah!" Will looked surprised. "You've never done anything that you knew was going to be hard but worth it?"

"No," Kenny said, abruptly tired. He looked at Will's computer again. "No. But your web designs are worth it. Are you going to go back to teaching?"

"Hmm...." Will closed his laptop again and put it into the case on the floor. Princess was sprawled next to it, trying to be a big fluffy pain in the ass, and without a hello or how are you, Will picked her up. Kenny was about to caution him, because she was sort of a diva, but before he could say anything, the cat was sprawled on his chest, licking his face. Bitch. He'd had fantasies....

"That wasn't an answer," Kenny said, pulling his drunken brain out of the pickle jar.

"I was just thinking," Will said, sighing softly. "I have a sub job tomorrow in the Grant district. I've got to remember to put on my armor, you know? The last time I subbed a middle school there, I caught a math book in the face."

"Jesus fucking Christ!"

Will pulled back a grimace. "Well, you know, not everyone's a nice guy, Kenny. Not everyone is you."

"I'm not that nice," Kenny said helplessly, because he wasn't. Inside, he was hoping Will never got another teaching job, because he thought Will should put all his talent somewhere else, and given Will had just told him he really loved the job, that wasn't nice at all.

"You're awesome," Will said sincerely. "Do you want to watch some TV?"

Kenny let out an absurd little whimper. "Can, uhm... you wouldn't mind if I snuggled, would you?"

With a shrug, Will opened himself up on the couch. "Yeah. You won't offend me. Knock yourself out."

Kenny grabbed the remote and started searching for the Syfy channel, and took up that extended arm. God. A het guy who liked to snuggle. He was totally wasted on women like whatserface, Kenny was sure of it.

As he let his eyes glaze over and his head loll on Will's shoulder, he was also sure that he had to do something really nice for this big guy who just seemed to want to make the world a better place.

"Come over Wednesday," he slurred. "We'll spend more time on the graphic novel, less time drinking."

He heard an extremely masculine grunt. "That there's a deal," Will said, and Kenny decided it could be his best breakup ever.

"SO THAT'S what you were doing when I saw you last May," Cara said thoughtfully, and Kenny grimaced.

"You must have seen Will then—because you and I didn't meet until—"

"Oh yeah." Cara crinkled her freckled nose. "So, Will—why didn't you tell him?"

Will looked away. "Well, you know. I just barely knew myself. Besides—I mean, I may have sort of fallen for him at first sight, but I'm slow. It took me a while to figure out what first sight really was."

"Yeah, Cara," Nina said archly. "Sometimes it takes someone a while to realize what first sight really is!"

Cara rolled her eyes. "Yeah, yeah, yeah... you were sneaky."

Kenny strangled a laugh. "Will is anything but sneaky. He was just clueless!"

"That's not true!" Will protested. The music had resumed, and for a moment he watched Ashley being whirled around by what looked to be an older cousin, and he envied her. He wasn't great at it, but he and Kenny had at least learned to dance. "I knew exactly what I was doing," he said with dignity, and Kenny raised an eyebrow in disbelief.

"And what's that, precious?"

Will grinned proudly. "I was making myself *indispensable*."

And in that moment, Kenny's smirky front fell away, and what was left was what Will thought of as the real Kenny. He was funny, yes, but he was also the same guy who cried at weddings.

"Oh," he said, sounding poleaxed. "Well, consider yourself 'mission accomplished.'"

Will grabbed his hand, too conscious of Kenny's vulnerability to even take advantage and keep making fun. "Well, you know. I do have a good idea every now and then."

CONFESSIONS AND CONFUSIONS

IT WAS sort of embarrassing to admit it, but Will's mommy was still his best friend—although after two weeks of visiting Kenny a couple of times a week, he thought maybe Kenny was starting to outrank her.

Will mowed his mommy's lawn every weekend. She'd never asked him to, but after his father had passed away, it became his job, and after he'd moved out, he'd continued to do it. She wasn't there all the time—in fact, she had enough volunteer projects that she was there maybe half the time—but when she *was* there, they often had lunch or went shopping or sometimes just sat and chatted, with no excuse needed whatsoever.

This Saturday was no exception to the lawn-mowing—or wouldn't have been if Sacramento wasn't having some bizarre, unprecedented three days' worth of muggy, icky rain in the middle of the weekend. Will was sort of depressed; he'd told Kenny he'd be over Sunday to mow his lawn too—he'd done it for the last two weeks, ever since Kenny's little "oopsie, I'm so *drunk*" episode. Kenny had cried on him that night. Even though Will had made plans to sleep over in case *he'd* gotten drunk, he'd changed his mind at the last moment because Kenny had seemed to need it so badly. The next morning... well, Will hadn't wanted to just ditch out on the guy. So he'd cooked breakfast, and made himself domestic, and talked to his new bestie some more.

And now Kenny's lawn needed mowing again, and even if it didn't, Will would need to find another reason to go. Kenny had gone in for his blood test this week, just to make sure Gif hadn't left him any nasty bugs Kenny hadn't been planning on, and Will thought he might like the moral support, but Will didn't want to seem like creepy guy who was always over either.

It was a delicate line to walk for someone who wasn't used to delicacy, really. But still, Will's standing appointment with his mother was not yielding so Will could waffle and flip-flop about Kenny.

Besides, although his mom *was* busy today, his aunt Cara was hanging out, watching her DVR, and the two of them sat down for lunch. This put a dash of awesome in Will's day, because Cara was hands down one of Will's favorite people.

He wasn't sure why he and Cara had always seemed to hit it off so well. He had clear memories of Cara just stopping by his house when he was a kid and saying, "You want to come play in the dirt with me?" And Will had gone. She'd always been working places where he could sit and play and tell stories to himself for hours, and unlike his father, who had wanted a better accounting of Will's time than that (football, track, starting his own business—*anything* was better than sitting around dreaming!), Cara thought there was nothing untoward about a little boy who liked to sing and play in the dirt.

And Cara had always seemed to make Will's *mom* happy. Whenever Anne Lafferty had gotten too grim, or too sad, or too stifled, living up to the many rules James Lafferty couldn't seem to live without, Cara would come over, grab Anne by the hand, and pull her and Will into an adventure. He remembered a summer Saturday that had ended up at the seashore simply because Cara had driven by and hauled the two of them outside and into her battered brown minivan. (She had a more recent model of that same car now—it was blue, but it was still beat to hell. Playing nice with her cars was not a virtue Cara had ever entertained.) In fact, he remembered a *lot* of things his mom and Cara had done on the spur of the moment, when his father had *never* believed in the spur of the moment. Although Will never suspected that his mother might not have been happy with his father (in fact, he was pretty sure they loved each other a *lot*), he did suspect that part of the reason his mom had been able to make that happiness stick, in spite of what seemed to be a whole lot of differences in personality, was Cara Dempsey.

So it was a gift to sit with Cara and eat in front of the television. One of Cara's passions was reality television shows, including the one they were watching, which featured guys in competing food trucks.

"Oh, gross," Cara said, tucking into a really amazing sub sandwich Will's mom had bought. Will's mom would do that—she knew Cara would be there since Cara didn't have cable, and she knew Will would be there, so she left a note saying food was in the fridge. It was sort of amazing, especially given that since his father had passed away, his mother didn't cook unless she really had to. In a way, Will wished she'd tell him to bring his own damned food, but he also knew she didn't mind entertaining.

"The sandwich?" Will asked after swallowing his bite, and Cara laughed, shaking her graying hair out of her face. She was actually only a few years younger than Will's mom, so in her midforties, but she wasn't a fan of hair dyes or makeup or anything artificial. That was okay—Will sort of loved her without all that.

"No, silly boy—the thing they're making on the show! Ew. Can you imagine trying to sell that?"

Will looked and shrugged. "I cook for myself all the time, Aunt Cara—I'm thinking I usually make worse than that."

Cara laughed. "Yeah, well, as long as you cook. I'm starting to think 'homemade' is anything not made at McDonald's."

Will laughed and took another heavenly bite. God—who didn't love Mr. Pickles? Especially when his mom was buying!

"Kenny likes it," he conceded.

Cara—whom he hadn't seen in a while—wrinkled her freckled nose. "Who's Kenny? He sounds like some kid you'd get in trouble for hanging around. Like that Jenkins kid who kept egging houses and blaming it on you!"

"Yeah, but me and Pete Jenkins were never friends," Will said, shuddering. God, Pete Jenkins—*there* was a reason to run fleeing through middle school. His favorite game had been to get behind Will and kick his back foot so Will would go sprawling. A lot of really average homework had gotten lost when that had happened. Talk about *gross*! "Kenny's a good guy," Will said stoutly, hoping the memory of a really good friend could make him forget middle school for the moment. "We're working on a graphic novel together."

"Yeah?" Cara perked up. She didn't have any particular artistic skills herself—except her skill with plants and gardening—but she did enjoy *looking* at art or visiting artists. Her house was filled to clutter with handcrafted wind chimes and hand-woven throws—she just appreciated the hell out of anything that involved a combination of imagination and regular household items.

"Yeah," Will said, feeling proud. "I mean, all I'm doing right now is subbing, and that goes away in June—"

"What about your web business?" Cara asked, and Will shrugged.

"It's been picking up. Oh, wait, here—" Will reached into his pocket and fumbled with his wallet. He produced one of the clever little business cards Kenny had made for him, with the computer that looked like a souped-up jalopy, complete with pinstripe and flames. "He got me a bunch of them, and I've handed them out. But it's weird. It's like, people I've never heard of keep calling me up because they've seen my business card. I've gotten three new clients!"

Cara looked at the card, her eyebrows arching in what Will thought was probably approval. "He made these for you?"

Will looked at the little card fondly. It had been really sweet, actually. Kenny had just thrown them on the coffee table and told him to take them, and then had sort of waved off Will's thanks.

"Yeah. See, I met him when he was breaking up with his boyfriend—"

Aunt Cara didn't say anything. She just looked up at Will as though he'd left a word out of a sentence.

Will flushed.

"Did, uhm, Mom tell you?"

Cara shook her head no. "Not in so many words. But she did tell me we should stop trying to pimp you out to my assistant. Was there anything *you* wanted to tell me, young William whom I love like a son?"

This was so much harder when he wasn't coming off the high of a three-hour masturbation bender. "I, well, I'm gay."

"All righty, then. So you're gay. Good to know. I've got some guys I can set you up with too."

Will's grin blossomed, slow and then wider and wider. "Not yet," he said, thinking that dating a guy would probably be just as awkward as dating a girl. "I'm sort of getting used to being in my own skin."

He was, actually, and it was *amazing*. He masturbated twice a day, three times on days he didn't see Kenny, and he'd watched every free Internet gay porn site available. Some of it was icky, some of it was creepy, and some of it was so damned hot he watched it twice. Oh. My. God. How could he have *had* a cock for twenty-eight years and never known that they were the best playground equipment known to man?

Cara tilted her head at him, smiling a little. "What's that like?" she asked, and she sounded like she really wanted to know for herself.

"It's... it's good," he said inadequately. It wasn't just the masturbation either. "It's like, like I know what I want. I used to look at girls and not feel anything and wonder what was wrong with me. Now I look at guys and I *want* them, and I feel like *nothing's* wrong with me, I'm *great*."

Cara looked thoughtful. "That's sort of awesome," she conceded. "I'm happy for you."

Will smiled. "Yeah?"

When she smiled, she was amazingly beautiful. "Yeah. Baby, I've always thought you had this just... transcendent person inside you, and you, I don't know, you hid him. Plain clothes, plain haircut, plain job. But I would *hear* you making up these worlds, telling yourself stories, and I thought, 'You know? This kid has some greatness in him. He just needs to let it out!' And you right there? You were *shining*, you were so happy."

Will's face heated and he took another bite of sandwich. "Thanks," he mumbled, trying not to spit out crumbs. "Mom seemed okay with it too."

"Well, you *are* the apple of your mommy's eye. She'll be rooting for you to hook up like a madwoman."

Nope. Blush not going away. "Well, right now it's all figurative. I'm doing lots of, uhm, homework, you know, into the, uhm, mechanics of—"

Cara was famous for her no-bullshit eye-level. "You're whacking off like it's a sport and you're training for the Olympics, aren't you?"

Will grinned, because you so rarely got to brag about something like this. "I'm about to get a bronze in the nationals and I'm hoping for a gold sometime in the next week."

Cara threw back her head and laughed, and they settled down to watch the Hawaiian team trounce the Chicago team on *Battle of the Sandwich Wagons* or whatever it was that Cara was invested in today.

By the time they were done eating, Mom had gotten home, and it took five minutes with Cara behind the remote control before they had settled into their televisional/conversational groove. Will had heard it and participated since he was very small, but he never tired of it.

"CeeLo—like the tat." That would be Aunt Cara, who could get away with saying words like "tat" without sounding like she was trying to be young and hip.

"But what if he ever wants to grow hair?" Will's mom said plaintively, and Cara sent her a blatant look of pity that fit right in rhythm. Deucalion padded from the back room like she'd said his name. "Like Deuc? I think he wants to grow hair, and it always feel so unfair."

"I'm thinking he will grow hair," Cara said patiently. "Except *unlike* Deucalion, hair is not a thing CeeLo wants to grow!"

"Don't be bitchy, Cara. It was only a question." Deucalion let out a devil *mreowl* and started rubbing back and forth against Will's mom's arm. He was affectionate, for all he looked like a giant scrotum, and Mom picked him up and cuddled him like he was Kenny's Princess.

Cara shuddered. She was the one who first noticed that the cat looked like a giant scrotum. "If you want to ask a question, ask whether or not Christina Aguilera shaves her coochie. That dress gets any shorter, we're gonna have a front-row seat."

"I'm not sure if I'm supposed to care or not about Christina Aguilera's coochie," Will said, wondering if that was a gay line in the sand he didn't know about.

For a moment Cara looked like she was seriously thinking about something, and then, as the pause was about to get important, she just shrugged. "Well, you know us gardeners: it's all about the bush."

Will laughed like he was supposed to, but he was aware, even as they settled into their banter, that maybe he wasn't the only one who was thinking seriously about lines.

BUT HE was not thinking about gardening *or* coochies the next day. In fact, he was mostly thinking about snapping Kenny out of his funk.

Help me, Kenny texted around eleven—just when Will was trying to figure out what excuse he could use to text Kenny, actually.

What's up?

I have nothing to do and I'm two seconds away from dressing up and finding a bar.

You have beer.

High-alcoholic beer leftover from the time Will accidentally got Kenny drunk.

For a pity fuck, Will! I'm single and depressed!

Oh shit. Will was *so* not ready to share Kenny with anyone, even if it was just a strange cock Kenny would never see again.

I'll be over in—Oh shit. Will was running out of gas money, and the rain had let up the night before. He had to ride his bike.—*thirty. No pity sex. You have more self-respect than that.*

Fine. What are we going to do instead?

Will had already showered, thank God, and now he was running around his bedroom shoving shit into a backpack—spare change of clothes, sweater, wallet with dwindling cash in it.

Do you have cash and gas?

Yes—I can spring for you.

I can pay my own food. Wanna go to the beach?

There was a pause then, a long one, and Will kept packing stuff in hope. Finally, as he was hovering at his threshold, his bicycle under his hand, his phone buzzed.

I'll pack a lunch. We'll get sodas out of town. Dillon's Beach is calling our name.

"Woo-hoo!" Will's holler of triumph probably woke all his neighbors, but Will was getting the hell out of Dodge.

AN HOUR later, after a quick stop at Safeway for ice, crackers, and sodas, they were buzzing down the road in Kenny's little smart car and Will was trying to be philosophical about having his knees up to his chin and feeling like a deformed beetle skittering on the smooth tarmac of Highway 80.

"So," Kenny said once they had the stereo on (White Stripes and Cage the Elephant—good traveling music), "what prompted this little excursion?"

Will looked at him in surprise, flipping his hair out of his eyes as he did so. It was getting long, and the side part thing made it flop in his face really damned quickly. "You did," he said, wondering if he should go back and check his phone to make sure. "You were talking about going out and getting laid out of depression—I mean, that's a *terrible* reason to get laid!"

Kenny snorted softly. "Well, *yeah*. But nobody's ever talked me out of it before!"

"That was their bad. Didn't you meet Gif in a club?"

"God. Yeah." Kenny accelerated and buzzed past a truck, which to Will looked like a mouse buzzing past a Triceratops. Poor little mouse. Run, you fearless little bastard, run! "Okay, so clubbing or drinking or whatever is a bad idea right now. I hear you. But the beach?"

Will remembered his aunt Cara yesterday and the way she used to just *arrive* and take him and his mom off to adventures. Yeah, sometimes the adventure was just to go help her pick out flowers or visit an art gallery in the foothills, but sometimes they ended up in Tahoe tracking down a plant on someone's property, or out on a llama farm looking at stool samples for acidity, or... hell, *anywhere*. And sometimes, the beach.

"My mom's best friend," he said, because hiding things was not in his nature. "She's... well, my dad was a good guy, but he wasn't really... *spontaneous,* you know? And my mom's best friend, she used to come by, like, once a month, or sometimes once a week, and just… just haul us off to an adventure. And sometimes, when we were lucky, the adventure would be by the ocean. So, you know, I wanted an adventure for you. Some place the hell out of Sacramento, you know? You can be a whole new person with whole new stress responses, right?"

Kenny cast him a sideways look and nodded. "Will?"

"Yeah?"

"You… has anybody told you you're sort of special?"

Will wrinkled his nose. "You mean like special ed? Because yeah, I got told that all the time, but I've got to tell you, those kids were really sweet—I took it as a compliment."

"No, asshole!" Kenny snapped, but his voice was sort of choked, so Will assumed he wasn't being mean. "I mean like you're a really good person. Like… you *are* that sweet. You *are* special. It's like… like I never used to believe in God before, except he made you knock over my trash can."

Will started laughing. "My aunt Cara's pagan. She'd say that Goddess made me knock over the trash can."

Kenny sniffed, and Will watched him struggle to make the moment lighter. Finally he smiled like a little bit of sunshine as they drove into the Bay City fog. "Yeah, well, the Goddess must have felt bad for me—that was one prime collection of dildos I was throwing away."

Will grinned, suddenly feeling like the heavy moment, the frightening one, had been left behind in the buzz of the car's engine. "You know. Think of it as a sacrifice to the Goddess. You got a better life in return, one free of that total douche bag."

Kenny grinned and cranked up the radio. The White Stripes' "Seven Nation Army" sort of roared out of the radio, and what the hell. Sometimes Will was as down for a musical ass-kicking as the next guy. He opened his window and Kenny did the same, and they belted out the lyrics, because that was what it felt like to be free.

WHEN THEY got to the beach, Will grabbed his backpack and helped Kenny with the snacks and the drinks. They set up an old beach blanket of Kenny's and an umbrella—because apparently Kenny was more sun sensitive than the underside of an albino lizard (Kenny's words, but Will could see it in the fairness of his skin)—and generally made themselves at home. Will had brought a paperback copy of Christopher Moore's *Sacré Bleu*, which he planned to read later, but first....

"What are you doing?" Kenny asked. He was in the process of sitting on the blanket, but as he watched Will rifle through his backpack, he stopped.

"I got this thing like two years ago," Will said excitedly, producing a little rainbow package of colored fabric. "I was going to fly kites when I worked at San Juan, but we had like, no wind for the entire week of the science project, which sucked because they were *making* kites, so I never got to use it."

"I forget," Kenny said, standing up fully and coming to peer over Will's shoulder as he unrolled the frameless kite from its little package. "You've got to know a hell of a lot to teach grade school."

Will nodded seriously. "Liberal studies—people laugh, you know. They're like 'liberal,' must be 'easy'—but you've got to be good at *everything* before you graduate, and then there's the credential, which is a whole other skill set, and...." He remembered his prospects for jobs at the moment, which mostly consisted of walking into other people's classrooms and doling out their emergency bookwork, because nobody expected a sub to have any skills at all. "And, anyway, lots of stuff that I'm not using at the moment because all I do is say, 'Your assignment's on the board. Ask me if you have any questions.' But see?" He gestured widely to blustery wind along the breakers. No power lines, no buildings, just sand and sea and a surprisingly small number of people, considering how clear the day was. "It's perfect. This baby can finally get some air time and fly!"

He turned and realized Kenny was, well, really close. His eyes— the pretty blue ones that Will had first noticed—were focused on his face like Will was being really wise, and in that moment Will felt fearless and important.

And turned-on.

In fact, he hadn't been this turned-on since Kenny had fallen asleep in his arms after Will had accidentally gotten him drunk. Oh man—Kenny was close enough for Will to feel his body heat now, but that night, when he was just warm and limp and powerful, leaning against his body....

Will was getting a stiffy.

He smiled gamely at Kenny and resisted the urge to close the gap between them—but oh man. Kenny's mouth was parted, and Will... he lowered his head slowly, forgetting about the kite in his hands, and then a gust of wind caught the rolled-up rice-paper tail and sent it flipping around the two of them. Will jerked his arms up to give it room so it didn't get tangled, and Kenny took a quick step back.

Well, damn.

But the kite tail was floating in the wind, and the little square frameless box kite was jerking in time. Will caught the spool of string before it could flip onto the sand, and let out about six feet of slack. The kite wove above them for a minute, and Will turned to Kenny with a grin, hoping his disappointment wouldn't show.

"Here—hold it for a sec. I'll take off my shoes and we can run down near the surf."

Kenny had worn flip-flops, which he kept on, but he held out his hands and Will took off his tennis shoes and socks, liking the texture of the sand between his toes. He grinned up at Kenny again and realized that Kenny was sort of fixating on Will's feet and calves, and he wondered if he had some deformity his mother had never told him about.

"Your legs are getting really defined," Kenny said out of the blue. "All that bike riding you're doing."

Oh yeah. Will shrugged, mostly to hide a blush. "I'm sort of loving the flexibility of working from home," he admitted. "Lots more physical activity—here, give me, and you don't have to—" He reached out again for the kite.

Kenny pulled back. "No! I want to fly it!" He unspooled some more string and the thing really took off. He had this smile, sort of an expression of absolute joy on his face that told Will that no, Will really wasn't a doofus and Kenny *wasn't* doing this to humor him. Will was doing something that made his friend happy.

And anything beyond friends? Well, that would have to wait— until *both* of them were ready for the fallout.

Still, that didn't stop Will from hanging back and watching as Kenny took the kite and went trotting quickly across the sand, the kite dancing overhead in his wake. His body was lithe and tight. Will had seen him in his underwear, and brother, did that muscular little body stand up to the exposure. Small muscles, defined, and a nice patch of neatly trimmed chest hair. Will didn't have a lot of body hair himself, but he sure did appreciate it on Kenny.

And he really wanted to appreciate it even more.

Then why didn't you kiss him, genius?

Because I didn't want to be some random hookup, moron! He was ready to hit the bars this morning—I could have been the Boston Strangler and he still would have offered to blow me.

Oh.

Yup, even Will's inner voice had to concede that he wanted more from this relationship. Yes, it would be his first gay kiss and his first gay sex, but that didn't mean he wanted it to be his *last* kiss and his *last* sex from this person.

Especially if the person happened to be Kenny, who really was starting to outrank Will's mom for that role of best friend forever.

THEY ATE sandwiches after their run, with the kite anchored by one of Will's shoes and flickering above them, and Will figured they'd probably get fast food on the way back. Then they sat quietly—Will brought out his book, and Kenny pulled out a battered copy of Stephen King's *It*, and they read, side by side, for about an hour. Every now and then Will would laugh and Kenny would say, "What?" Will would read him a passage from the undoubtedly brilliant Christopher Moore, and the oddest part of that was that Kenny would *laugh*. Usually Will had to explain Moore to people—even his mom and aunt Cara. Hell, even his fellow *teachers* hadn't gotten the biting satire, but Kenny? Kenny laughed. It was about the best sound in the world, kind of high and dry and sarcastic—but warm too.

On the way home, Kenny surprised him and stopped in the city. They went to the wharf and had the big sourdough bowls filled with clam chowder while they walked to the end of the pier and looked out at the bay.

Will huddled in his sweatshirt, cold, and looked at Kenny, who was doing the same in a thin hoodie, but neither of them wanted to leave.

"I just want a future," Kenny said suddenly, without preamble. But Will didn't even have to guess what he was talking about. They were here because of his breakup, after all.

"I know you do," Will said with feeling. "So do I."

"You want my future?" Kenny asked, one side of his mouth quirking.

Will rolled his eyes. "It's just… I mean, I'm pretty sure I'll find a teaching job by the end of the summer, it's just… it would be nice to have some control over it, right?"

"Yeah, but you do have control over your own business," Kenny said, and Will grimaced. Of all the things he and Kenny seemed to agree on, Will got the distinct impression that going back to teaching was not one of them.

"I do—and it's picking up. It's just… solid. Predictable—that's not a bad thing in a job. I know it's not bright and shiny, but then, I'm not really a bright-and-shiny person, you know that."

"What?" Kenny said, and he sounded a little shocked.

Will shrugged. "Well, look at me—I'm not setting the world on fire here. I just wanted a little niche, right? Me, my classroom, my kids—a chance to do something worthwhile, something that will last."

Kenny grunted. "That's bullshit," he said with surprising passion. "You *are* bright and spectacular. You *can* set the world on fire. That novel we're doing? That's—"

"Those are your pictures, Kenny."

"That's *your* inspiration, idiot. Your websites? Those are amazing—they're user-friendly, you have a great sense of graphic placement, and your prose should win you advertising awards. Seriously—you have so much more to offer than just teaching—"

"Well, thank you," Will said, trying to find the reason for his hurt. "I just thought that teaching was important."

Kenny sighed. "It is important—"

"Besides," Will interrupted because he didn't want to hear the "but" he sensed coming, "we're talking about *your* future. And maybe before you go out and start looking for your future in another Gif, you might want to figure out why Gif wasn't the right guy."

"I know why Gif wasn't the right guy," Kenny sighed, and some of the fight went out of him. "Gif wasn't the right guy because I was looking for the wrong things in him."

"Yeah? What were you looking for?" Will wanted to take notes.

"I was looking for sparkly," Kenny said, staring out over the bright bay. "I should have been looking for warm and real."

Oh, that was encouraging. Those were two qualities Will could *do*.

"I think that's a great start," Will said with fervor, and Kenny was standing close enough for Will to drape an arm over his back and pretend it was all in the name of being a buddy.

"AND YOU didn't kiss him?" Cara asked bluntly.

Nina sat by her side with an almost identical expression of disbelief. "Yeah, seriously. Nobody made a move? You were in San Francisco, for sweet Christ's sake!"

"He wasn't ready yet," Will said, at the same time Kenny said, "I wasn't ready yet."

Will grinned at him, and Kenny looked embarrassed.

"Are we getting to the part where one of you *was* ready?" Cara asked. "Because seriously—it's a nice story and all, but I want to dance at my wedding!"

"We're getting there," Will promised. "I swear."

ALMOST READY

KENNY GOT the results of his HIV test e-mailed to him, which meant he was at work when he saw the result.

His first impulse was to stand up and Safety Dance all over his little cubicle with its *Firefly* posters and Harry Potter memorabilia. (Gif hated that shit, which was why it lived in Kenny's cubicle.)

Kenny looked up and saw Cam, the guy on the other side of his cubicle, working steadily on the pamphlet he was designing for an in-house change of policy. Kenny got to design the packaging graphics for the new product, which was a definite improvement when it came to job assignments, and he was never sure how to act around Cam. Cam—fiftyish, jowly, and on his third wife—got there early and left early, using the flex time with interest so he could coach his kids' sports teams and spend time with them in spite of the fucked-up family situation. Kenny's dad had always been too busy running his own business, and his mom taught high school, so they'd never been able to do that. Kenny sort of admired the guy for his dedication, but he felt bad shooting over his head like that.

"What's up?" Cam noticed him wiggling in his chair, and Kenny fought a brief battle for candor. No one at work even knew he was gay yet—he'd spent his first few months trying so hard to be a wunderkind that he'd sort of pretended he didn't have a personal life.

"Got some good news," he said vaguely.

Cam raised his eyebrows, but Kenny was *so* not spilling the whole story, not right now.

Cam sighed and then shrugged. "Well, you know. Find someone you *want* to talk to and celebrate."

Kenny felt bad for a minute. "It's no big deal, really," he lied. God, the big negative—it was what every sexually active boy wanted to hear, wasn't it? "But thanks, I'll take your advice."

Cam grunted. "Great. I'll dispense it when needed." And then he turned back to his project, leaving Kenny feeling *more* than a little guilty. Okay, now that he'd proved he was a wunderkind—and sacrificed his relationship to do it—maybe it was time to stop being a big glittery meteor in the work world and maybe start being a human being. Because God knew, with Will as his conscience, he wasn't going to go out and bag himself a pretty new boyfriend—not anytime soon, that was for damned sure.

Will. Of course—*duh*. Kenny reached into his pocket for his phone and noticed that Cam's soda—the same kind Will drank—was on its last inch in the bottle. Okay, first he'd text Will and make sure he was coming over for the evening, and then he'd get Cam a soda and maybe start being a real person at work.

And *then* he'd plan dinner.

"So do you want me to bring takeout?" Will asked over the phone, and Kenny smiled indulgently, stirring the sausage in one pot before moving to the tomato sauce in the other. It was very Will to offer to bring food when Kenny *knew* his finances had to be hurting. Will was considerate like that.

"Nope," Kenny said proudly. "I'm making dinner tonight. Cleaned off the table, set it, everything." He'd even bought ice cream. "Bring yourself, your laptop, and your appetite, Daddy is cooking tonight!"

Will's laugh was that same warm, sunshiny sound Kenny had learned to appreciate during the past month. *God*, he was good company. "What's the occasion? I need to know what to wear."

Anything. Cargo shorts, T-shirt, jeans, T-shirt, corduroys, no shirt, polyester plaid—I could look at your big bear body in anything.

Oh God. Kenny promptly told his baser self to stand down, Straight Boy was *not* for him. "Nothing fancy," he said firmly into the phone. "And the occasion is, if you must know, I got my second HIV test back, and I am clean, clear, and damned near virginal. Huzzah and hip hooray, at least Gif could use a rubber."

There was a startled pause on the other end of the line, and then Will's sincere voice. "That's *awesome*," he said. "I'll have to bring something!"

"No, no, no, no, no—you're missing the point. The point is *I treat you*, because baby, I got it going on. Pasta, homemade sauce, ice cream, pie, beer, Dr Pepper"—because Will drank it by the case— "salad, uhm—"

"Garlic bread?" Will prompted gently.

"*Dammit!*" Because sure enough, *that* was what Kenny had forgotten.

"I'll be over in half an hour. And seriously, Kenny. Congratulations. That must be sort of a load off your mind."

Yeah, a big viral load! But Kenny couldn't joke about it—not with Will, who had been kind and decent and a really good friend. "Yeah. I… I mean, part of the fun of being in a committed relationship is you know where you stand there, you know? And it's just nice to know I can move on."

"That's awesome. I'm really happy for you," he said, but the pronouncement was followed by the sort of loaded pause that sounded like it was full of words in Will's head.

"What?" Kenny asked. He didn't always get an answer when he asked that.

"Nothing," Will said, all of the hesitation gone. "I'll see you in a bit."

Will rang off and Kenny turned the heat off the sausage and onions, sneaking a bite before he added them into the sauce. He wanted it to be perfect; Will Lafferty of the shrinking white belly (he'd been working out and riding his bike since he got fired) had been a *godsend* in the past month.

Kenny's college dating had been… well, sort of exploitative. Or exploited. It just felt like every guy had six other guys he wanted to bang besides Kenny, and every time Kenny thought they were getting to the point where the rubbers could come off, he'd find out the other guy had just been in a three-way with all of Kenny's exes, and *bam!* Kenny was club-fucking again. Gif had been Kenny's first move at cohabitation and his first attempt at a real relationship. Besides just the fucking *betrayal*, there was that horrible sense of failure, of impending doom, that "I'll never have somebody to love" that went with a failed relationship.

Will had helped Kenny get past that.

For one thing, for all that he looked like a refrigerator (and the more comfortable he got around Kenny, the more gracefully he moved), his mind was incredibly quick. Once he'd started unloading his character bible, Kenny had realized that Will had entire *worlds* of layered depth, of pathos, of creativity, lying beneath that broad-faced surface. Sitting there making preliminary sketches, listening to Will's ideas on layout, on plot arc, on which graphic elements to stress to make the ending more impactful, Kenny became lost in their idea, their steampunk galaxy, complete with rocket-powered giant-wheeled tricycles and giant sentient house cats made of metal. The characters too, a man and a woman, were fascinating, culpable, flawed, and ultimately heroic. Kenny felt like he'd known them after the past weeks, like they were people he'd grown up with, and they'd gotten to star in this little drama because they were worthy.

He'd never drawn so well in his life.

It was *amazing*, how well he could draw, how many sketches he could produce with his computer stylus, just *listening* to Will detail what a scene was about. He'd never been a cooperative learner, had always disdained groups in school, sprawling in his desk and listening to the planners plot while he simply produced artwork on command to save (in his opinion) their lame ideas.

But Will—Will *brought it*. Kenny wouldn't have been able to do *any* of the stuff he was doing now without Will's dynamic, creative ideas.

So that was one reason to be grateful to the big guy.

The other reason was more… complex.

He was just such a *nice man*. Kenny did snarky—he *got* snarky. But Will was just so… so… *sweet*.

Kenny didn't have a whole lot of memories of that night Will had accidentally gotten him drunk, but what he did have reflected pretty awesomely on Will. The end, he seemed to recall, was lying on Will and watching *Orphan Black* and crying all over Will's solid, straight-boy chest, the big ugly kind of cry, while Will just patted him gently on the back and told him it would all be okay.

Kenny didn't know how to thank him for that.

How did you thank someone you just met for actually *being* the "I love you, man!" man? The guy who would listen to you whine and complain and then stay the night and make you toast to eat with your painkillers and giant ice water? How did that guy even exist?

The morning after Kenny's little super-hoppy beer indulgence, he'd nibbled on his toast and said, "Too bad you didn't go away to college. You would have been *very* popular in your dorms!"

Will had shrugged and started pan-frying some canadian bacon he'd found in Kenny's refrigerator. "I wasn't this comfortable in my own skin," he said frankly. "It wasn't until—never mind."

"No!" Kenny protested, and he didn't even wince. "C'mon—you heard my worst day *ever*. Tell me yours?"

Will had stayed the night, and he'd actually packed for it that time. He was wearing a clean pair of sleep shorts and a T-shirt and flip-flops on what must have been size-fifteen feet. He kept his back turned long enough for Kenny to read *I Aim To Misbehave* on the back and feel stupid because he hadn't even spotted the *Firefly* reference. Briskly, Will started plating up the canadian bacon and some fruit salad he'd opened. He set it down in front of Kenny without speaking—and without even making eye contact—and Kenny was just about to totally apologize for whatever it was he'd just dredged up when Will said, "My father died." And then he sat down and looked at his food.

"Oh Will—"

"See, he wasn't a bad guy, but he wasn't… I mean, he wasn't a communicator. I used to stay up late with my ear pressed against the wall because I could hear my mom talking to him. She'd tell him things like 'Will got an A in science today!' and my dad would say, 'Smart kid.' But he never said those things to *me*."

Kenny opened his mouth, and closed it, and opened it, and then, at a total loss, put his hand on Will's as it hovered over his fork.

Will shot him a brief smile. "So anyway, suddenly, all that—you know, that *fear* you feel, about 'Does this person like me, or what if he thinks I'm an asshole, or what if I'm so totally weird and off the grid

I'll need to be committed'—that just went the hell away, you know? It wasn't even a consideration anymore. I just… just scattered it with my dad's ashes, let the tide wash it away. And didn't let it bother me anymore."

Kenny found himself smiling, just *smiling* at Will, his mouth stretched so wide his teeth dried out. "That's fucking amazing," he said, meaning every syllable. "No bitterness, no angst—you have much to teach me, Master!"

Will winked. "Eat your crappy breakfast, Padawan, and show me where the lawn mower is. Your ex took care of the lawn, didn't he?"

Kenny had done laundry while Will mowed his lawn, and Kenny tried not to yearn for the sweet straight boy who had literally knocked his shit over on the first day.

It got harder every time they met in the evening to work on their little project.

Will got a few sub jobs in the local district—sometimes he met Kenny after work, looking serious and blocky in the semiprofessional uniform of the public school teacher. On the days he *didn't* teach, he wore funny T-shirts and cargo shorts (since it was May in the Sacramento Valley) and he looked *fun*. He smiled more on those days, Kenny thought with a pang. He needed to do something besides teaching. Kenny remembered all of his teachers—and they'd been nice people. But their whole job was to teach people what shape the box was.

Kenny didn't like to think of Will locked in the box. He wanted Will *out* of the box.

The Monday after Will mowed his lawn, Kenny designed and ordered five hundred business cards. Will Lafferty, Web Designer, with the important information on the back and a bold, brightly colored graphic of a computer on fire with the *good* pinstriped motorcycle kind of flames. Kenny was damned good at what he did—instead of looking tacky, they'd made Will look cutting edge and powerful. He'd only given Will 250 of the cards, because he had a feeling they'd sit on Will's desk while the man who could make *pest control* look glamorous (Kenny had since made him take that business down as his sample) dithered with "But really, I'm sort of a little mudfish in a big koi pond" and refused to put himself forward.

Instead, Kenny had taken fifty of those cards and put them on the desk of everyone on his floor of the building, and kept the rest of them to pass out to anyone who needed one.

So far Will had garnered three new clients, and from what those guys were telling Kenny at work, they'd never been happier with their website maintenance or setup. Kenny didn't tell him—for some reason, he just wanted to see Will smile.

For some reason, my ass!

God. Kenny puttered around his kitchen, checking the pasta, chopping the greens for the salad, adding the pine-nut ranch dressing, and trying to avoid the inescapable truth.

He just wanted Will period.

Kenny, Kenny, Kenny... he's not even your type!

True—he preferred men with legs up to their chins and narrow faces with chiseled cheekbones. But maybe seeing Gifford, who had a narrow face with chiseled cheekbones, being nailed by Oscar, who at least had the chiseled cheekbones, made Kenny think twice.

Maybe he just wanted a guy who made him feel good about himself and shared his passions and *mowed his fucking lawn* without complaining all the goddamned time.

Wow.

Settling much, Kenny?

No, he told himself grouchily. He'd settled for Gif. Will was way out of his league.

And he's straight!

And—oh, hey, he's here!

Kenny answered the door with a genuine smile and some gratitude. Will had gotten fresh garlic and real butter with the fresh sourdough round, because there was no such thing as diet when garlic bread was on the table.

He wore a T-shirt that said *Party on, Wayne. Party on, Darth* and featured Lego figures of Bruce Wayne and Darth Vader, and Kenny couldn't seem to stop giggling over it as he set the table.

"God, you're easy," Will said, winking at him, and all the pep talks in the world couldn't make Little Kenny stand down. *He has no idea.*

"So, I hear you got a new client," Kenny said, suddenly unable to keep that a secret anymore. "Here, sit down. I just need to pull stuff off the stove."

Will grinned at him and settled in the chair farthest from Kenny's path around the kitchen. "Yeah—that was nice of you. Apparently you wallpapered your office with business cards—thanks!" He gnawed his lip. "I'm worried, though. That one guy—the sort of douchey one who wants to convince everyone he's, like, a world-class fisherman—"

"Ward?"

"Yeah, that guy. Anyway, he wants something 'new and exciting,' which means he wants new graphics and not just the stuff I can buy off the regular sites—"

"I can design stuff for you!" Kenny said excitedly, thinking it could be something else they could work on. The pasta was already tossed in a pretty ceramic bowl, and he set that down on a hot pad. He pulled the salad out of the refrigerator and set it down beside the pasta while Will kept talking.

"Yeah, but Kenny—how much do you charge? I mean, I feel bad enough taking your time for the business card—"

"That was a gift!" Kenny protested, and Will nodded vehemently, taking away the sting.

"I know—and I'm so grateful." Will rearranged the stuff on the table to give Kenny room to put the milk. "It's awesome—you actually made *me* look cool, and that's some doing! But taking your talent without paying you back isn't something I can do."

Kenny shrugged and pulled the garlic bread out of the oven. "Well, then, pay me. Tell me what the regular graphics places charge and then tell me what you want. We'll come up with something special and I'll take my cut. It's no big deal."

Will's smile suddenly turned shy. "Yeah?" he asked, and if Kenny didn't know better, he'd say the big man was flirting with him.

Kenny smiled back and found himself blushing. "Yeah," he said. "I like working with you."

And smile? Did Kenny think that first expression was a "smile"? Because this one here opened Will's face up and flooded the world with sunshine. Oh holy jebus, *that* was a smile!

"Awesome!" Will crowed. "And"—he flushed a little, the color easy to read on his wide, smooth-skinned face—"and honestly, I have some ideas."

Kenny sort of loved him more for that. It not only meant he was being genuine about not wanting to take advantage, but he also appreciated Kenny's talent too.

"We'll talk about it after dinner," he said. He cut the bread quickly and put it in a wooden bowl with a nice linen towel on top, and then set that down in front of Will.

He started serving and realized Will was just gazing at him with admiration. "Look at all the *stuff* you've got!" he said in wonder. "Arty bowls, tablecloths and place mats, pasta spoons—wow! Your whole kitchen is just done in grown-up! How does that happen to someone our age?"

Kenny waved his hand and tried for casual. "It's the gay," he said, trying not to preen too much. He actually got his liking of nice things from his parents. *They* went for very *Better Homes and Gardens*, because that was just the whole of Davis, but he liked eclectic and funky cool as a substitute. "All gay men come with a home decorator card, didn't you know that?"

Will looked at him with a twist to his mouth—one of the few times Kenny had seen his expression less than open. "I sincerely doubt it," he said drily. "I'm pretty sure it's you—and I definitely like it."

Kenny had no idea something without sexual innuendo could make him blush, but sure enough, his face heated and his hand grew slippery on his milk glass. He was suddenly glad he'd opted out of wine.

"What makes you think so?" he asked, looking down at his plate. He needed to take a bite of spaghetti, but he was painfully aware he'd put on a date shirt and taken off his apron. He didn't want pasta on his date shirt, did he?

"Well, because you're *you*," Will said enthusiastically. "You've got an eye for things, for weird combinations that go together. Like that bowl, the indigo and the plain terra-cotta—that's it, right? Terra-cotta?"

Kenny looked up at him and tried a real smile, but his throat swelled up painfully instead. Will hadn't said a word about the little gift Kenny had left on his shoes. Not *one word*. Kenny didn't know what that meant—or he *did* know what that meant, and at the same time it made Will an *amazing* friend to hang out with, it made him a really shitty one to fall in love with.

Not love. He's a friend.

"Yeah," he said quietly. "Terra-cotta." He was good at making things light—time to do that. "So how do you know it's not the gay?"

It was Will's turn to flush. For a moment he busied himself with his food, digging into his spaghetti and using the most excellent bread to sop up the sauce. He ate quietly and then looked up. Kenny had taken a bite himself in the intervening time, but when he'd finished chewing, he was still looking at Will, waiting patiently for an answer.

What he got was another question instead.

"Okay, so you know that bag you left on my shoes?"

Without ceremony or parachute, Kenny's heart dropped into his balls and his balls dropped to the floor. "Uhm, yeah."

"Can you be gay if you only use some of what was in there?"

Kenny blinked and tried to remember *exactly* what had been in that incriminating little bag. "You can be gay even if you don't use *anything* that was in there," Kenny said, some of his embarrassment and anxiety giving way to confusion. "Why?"

Will's expression turned inward and he gave sort of a sweet, simple smile. "Oh!" he said. "Good—that's a load off my mind. Thanks!"

And with that he started ripping into his food with his usual enthusiasm, leaving Kenny floundering. He'd promised not to pry, hadn't he? He'd... he'd promised himself not to pressure the guy! But... he just couldn't *leave* it there, right? Just... he... omigod....

"*Will!*" Kenny said, his voice strangled.

Will looked up from his spaghetti guilelessly, a hunk of bread in his mouth. "Whmf?"

"Was there anything *else* you wanted to ask me?"

Will's big brown eyes made one of those careful explorations for the secrets of the universe that might possibly lie in the interior of his mind. They rolled left, then right, then down, then right, and then they looked at Kenny again.

"Well, that, uhm, that plug thing?"

Kenny slurped in a noodle and spattered sauce all over his face *and* his unexpected date shirt. "Yeah?" he said, wiping his face off with his napkin.

"Do they have anything… *smaller*? 'Cause I clench up when I look at that thing."

Kenny closed his eyes and sucked on the end of the napkin, getting it thoroughly wet. Behind his eyes, the vision of Will naked, lying on a bed with his thighs spread, making tentative forays with the butt plug, repeated like an X-rated GIF.

"There, uhm," he murmured, "are *no* plugs smaller than that one." He dabbed at his shirt with the wet end of the napkin. "Uhm, if you think about how men are, uhm, built, *nobody* is smaller, uhm, in the *penile* area, than that plug."

Will stopped chewing for a moment, and his eyeballs did that careful exploration for the secrets of the universe again. "Oh. *Oh. Ooooohhh.* Okay. I mean, I looked at the pictures and all, but, you know, the plug just looks bigger in life than the picture of the, erm, penile things, even the big ones like mine."

Oh God. Kenny wrapped his hand around his milk glass. When his fingers didn't touch, he looked up at Will and tried not to swallow his tongue. "Uhm, how big a, erm, *penile* thing are you talking here, Will?" And omigod! The secrets of the universe were *not* right beyond Kenny's right shoulder!

Will looked at the milk glass and then wrapped *his* hand around it. He had really big hands—his finger and thumb touched and overlapped a little. Will squinted one eye, adjusted his hand, and pulled his thumb and forefinger apart so they weren't quite touching. Then he eyeballed the height of the glass and stroked his hand unmistakably up until it hovered about two inches over the brim.

Kenny's mouth went dry, and he fumbled for a drink of milk, knocking his glass over and sloshing milk all over his plate, and he still didn't really notice until his lap grew chill and clammy.

"Uhm, is that *you*? Because, uhm, Will, most men aren't built that way."

Will looked up from a contemplation of his fingers, because apparently his approximate cock size was not close enough to real-life for him, and frowned. "Kenny—man, you're getting milk on your nice clothes. Here, forget about my stupid question. You go change and I'll clean up and serve you again, okay?"

"Oh—oh *shit*! Okay." He stood up and sopped some of the milk with the napkin and then dropped it in his plate and fled.

He spent the next five minutes going from old jeans to second-date outfit to yoga pants and a T-shirt and then back again, asking himself what in the hell he thought he was doing. Of course, every time he thought he had a handle on the fact that he was having dinner with a *friend*, he'd remember that suggestive hand and his milk glass and start looking for his *really* good dating clothes, because… *dayum*.

"Don't dress for me!" Will hollered down the hall as though he knew *exactly* what Kenny was doing. "I promise not to scare you with any more penile questions!"

Kenny buried his face in one of his big, fluffy hypoallergenic pillows in a three-hundred-thread-count blue-and-gold pillowcase, and screamed. Oh God. *This* was his life? He should just go out there, make his apologies to Will, and explain that he couldn't hang out anymore because he needed to get back into the dating scene *right the fuck now*.

But… but he *couldn't*. He was having so much fun! *They* were having so much fun! He hated to admit it, because it sounded so lame, so syrupy, but he was having a better time with Will *sans* sex than he'd had with Gif *with* the sex. He couldn't remember the last time he'd put himself out to cook for Gif; Gif would prefer to go out and dance. But Will—he really liked that table setting and the fresh sauce. He'd stopped and gotten the good bread and the real butter and garlic. Gif would have brought home the sliced stuff, probably not even sourdough, and margarine. And Will didn't *expect* Kenny to do anything for him—but he was damned grateful for what Kenny did. *God*, it was the best relationship Kenny had ever had—now if only Kenny could stop fantasizing about what William Lafferty looked like naked!

He finally picked yoga pants and an old T-shirt and went down the hall feeling irritated, embarrassed, and *hungry*. By the time he got back, Will had washed off his plate, run the garbage disposal, and replated his meal. To Kenny's surprise, he'd opened a bottle of wine Kenny had out on the counter and poured Kenny a glass of that as well.

Kenny sat down (there was a spare dishtowel on his seat to sop up any extra milk) and smiled sheepishly. "Sorry—I'm not usually so clumsy."

Will shrugged, also a little sheepish. "I was being inappropriate at the dinner table," he said gravely. "Didn't mean to freak you out."

"No, no," Kenny said, actually talking through his food because he didn't want anything to happen to it before he ate it. "My bad. I just hope you don't think all men are, you know, made like, uhm, *you* are, apparently." Good—only one "uhm"—he was improving. And he'd managed to take a few good bites of dinner too!

Will laughed a little and shook his head. "Yeah, well, it's not a gift if it doesn't get used," he said wisely. And then he pinked like he'd remembered that he *had* used the gift. Kenny was glad. Maybe all he'd done was give the guy stroke material, but he seemed happy about it, and that was sort of wonderful.

Kenny turned the topic to other things, and after they washed up, they sat down at Kenny's wooden coffee table. Will got out his laptop and spent time on the story, making comments to Kenny when he changed or added or wrote more in the arc. Kenny did the preliminary sketches for the next few pages in the comic, and Will filled in the dialog for him. The two of them worked so fluidly, Kenny had difficulty believing he'd never worked with the guy before.

They looked up after two hours of solid work and laughed, then stood and stretched. Princess made one of her rare appearances, coming out from between the couch and the end table so she could rub against Will's calf.

Will reached down to scratch her under the chin, and Kenny turned toward the kitchen. "You stay there and keep her happy—I'll be right back with dessert."

"Dessert?" Will said happily. "What are we having?

And again, Kenny was swamped with a wave of gratitude. Gif had whined about dessert and the weight he put on and how long he had to work out to get it off. Will knew he was big—he worked out—but by God, he ate *pie*. For all his self-deprecating geekdom, Will Lafferty knew how to *live*.

"Cherry pie," Kenny said primly. He could be the only one who knew that there was a dirty joke in there somewhere, but that was fine too.

"Ice cream?" Will asked hopefully, and then he grunted, which told Kenny without turning around that he'd hefted Princess into his arms, long white hairs or no.

"Vanilla," Kenny gloated. Oh, yes. It was nice to cook for a man who liked to eat, and Kenny's man liked to eat!

And then he realized what he'd just said in his head, and wished he had a time-out so he could kick his own ass. He busied himself with pie and cream (heh) some more, and Will called to him from the living room.

"Hey, Kenny!"

"What?"

"What are we going to do with this when it's done?"

And that reminded him, he had something he wanted to talk about!

"Actually, did you want to start posting it on the web?"

"Uhm, money?" Will said, and Kenny returned with two dishes of pie and ice cream. God, the cherry pie had turned out perfectly—actual cherries, not canned, and every bite was tart and sweet and basically an orgasm on a fork. Kenny was ready to come!

"Well, have you seen Kickstarter? Or any of the other websites that ask for money?" Kenny carried the pie into the living room and set it down on the coffee table, then gestured Will to put the cat down and enjoy.

Will grunted when Princess dropped on his foot, and then complied. "Does that ever work? I mean—"

"Well, yeah." He took his own bite and closed his eyes. Mm-*mm!* "But we don't even have to do that. Look, we've got two chapters done here. I've got a server and some space already—we use that, you design the website, and we post the first chapter. We do some promotions, we post a few pages regularly every week, and if we get enough interest, we start selling merchandise and ad space. When we get done with the first volume, we find a printer and sell the book—"

"So Internet self-publishing?" Will asked, sounding impressed. Kenny wanted to pat his cheek. All of this creative impetus, no marketing savvy whatsoever. Well, it was nice to bring something to the table.

"Exactly. And, you know—we won't make Sac Horror in September, but if we get enough interest, we can design enough merchandise to sell at SacAnime in January."

Will looked embarrassed. "I... okay, those web clients were helpful, and I *may* be able to pay my rent, but... but I can't front you any money for that, Kenny. God... I mean, it sounds *great*, but I hate going into business with you when I don't have anything to offer—"

"Besides the story idea?" Kenny asked, at a loss. "Come *on,* Will! I can write most of this stuff off on my taxes! I *know* people who've done this before. Hell, I know people who quit their day jobs to do this before!" Bless James and Rebecca of Lunasea Studios— their Little Vampires should be on every lunchbox in the country. "Not that I want to quit my day job, but... you know. We've spent our whole lives looking at this stuff from the outside and going 'Oo!' Wouldn't it be great if we could take an idea to the inside and see it from there?"

Will grinned, looking uncertain. "Well... I mean, I do. I'd *love* to do this and see it to the end and see something happen. But...."

"You've got the whole arc written, baby," Kenny said with a reassuring smile. "I mean...." Oh God, the thing he was most afraid of. "You know, unless you think you might find a girlfriend and want to drop me as a friend—"

"*No!*" Will said with gratifying swiftness. "No. For starters—girlfriend? I know you spilled your milk, but if nothing else, wipe the girlfriend idea off the board. Not gonna happen. And...." He looked away and wiggled like a schoolkid, then took a bite of pie and ice cream like he was covering his discomfort. "I *like* hanging out with you," he said, peeping shyly at Kenny from the corners of his eyes. "You're... you're like the friend I always wanted and never thought I could have!"

Kenny grinned, so pleased he could only celebrate it with another bite of pie. Okay, who needed a boyfriend? For the first time in his life, Kenny was enjoying the journey with another human being with no carrot attached at the end. That didn't mean he couldn't date someone else, right? He could have everything—this person he could share his day and his passion with, and a warm body in his bed. Hell, he'd had offers ever since Gif had bailed.

Of course, none of them were *Will*, but....

"You're my best friend too," Kenny said seriously. "Okay—I know someone at work who does contracts. He can draw up some no-muss contracts for us with each other, and I'll get you the domain name, okay? You can start designing the website, and we'll keep working together a couple of nights a week, but only now, we'll have an endgame in mind. You think?"

Will nodded and took another bite of pie. He spent a few minutes rolling a cherry around in his mouth before crunching down on it, and Kenny spent those few minutes watching him in agony. *And I can spend at least one night a week looking to go out and get laid,* he told himself. *Because I'm going to have to pound spikes for most of the night to get rid of this wood.*

Will finished torturing Kenny with unconscious food porn and nodded. "Okay. Excellent, in fact." He smiled gently, and Kenny almost moaned. Gentleness. God, since *when* had he looked for gentleness in a lover? "I'm glad you thought of the contract thing. Those make stuff really cut-and-dried—I don't want to ever lose you because of hurt feelings and the business."

Kenny took a bite of ice cream and thought mournfully that he might not be able to finish his piece. "Yeah," he said gruffly. "Hurt feelings would be a shitty reason to lose a friend."

CARA SNORTED inelegantly. "Well, weren't you two dumber than a bag of diapers?"

Kenny looked at Will and rolled his eyes. "Most oblique come-on *ever.*"

Will blushed and grimaced at all of them. God, they didn't have to act like it was *all* his fault that he hadn't read Kenny's signals right!

"Hey—in my defense, I'd never had to come on to a guy before!" he protested. "The girls just sort of—"

"Followed you home," Kenny supplied, his voice more arid than the outer reaches of space. "I know."

Will stuck out his tongue. "Well, yeah—I was sort of thick. But hey, I was *not* the idiot who—"

"Oh no," Kenny said, all playfulness dropping from his shoulders. The look he sent Will was now profoundly apologetic. "This part— God, Will! It's so *embarrassing*!" he complained, and Will took a *little* bit of pity on him and leaned over to kiss his cheek.

"Only a little," he said soothingly. "And you have to admit, it makes me look like sort of a hero."

Kenny's smile held no cynicism at all. "You *are* my hero," he said sincerely.

Will preened. "Well, you know. That's how we'll tell the story."

"Wait," Nina said like she'd just done some math. "Was that the graphic novel *we* bought when Anne took us to the convention?"

Cara did a double take. "*That's* what you're worried about now?"

"Here." Kenny reached into his pocket before Will could even think about it. "I'll bet you Will forgot to give you one of these, didn't he?"

The two women glared at Will reprovingly.

"They're family!" he protested, blushing, and Cara shook her head while she took the business card with the little oversexed fuzzy alien on it.

"We're *fans*, honey. Give us the skinny!"

"Check the website for dates and times—we're scheduled to do three more conventions in the next two months." Kenny looked at Will and waved his hand. "Well, go on, hero! I want to hear you tell it like you were meant to shine!"

Aw, geez. Who could resist with an invitation like that?

DICK OF STEEL

WILL'S MOTHER had these impeccable Old World According to June Cleaver manners—it drove him bugshit.

"Mom, I can pour—"

"No, hon, you just sit there and relax—I'll get the iced tea."

"But you didn't let me clean up after—"

"But I like doing dishes!"

"*But you worked all day!*"

His mother just smiled at him beatifically as he balanced on the wobbly bench at the picnic table she kept in her tiny backyard. "Oh, honey—don't worry about it."

He gritted his teeth. It was a holdover, he knew, from the days before she owned her own business, when his dad was alive. In those days she'd gone and worked full days for an insurance company and then come home and taken him to whatever sorry excuse for an extracurricular activity he'd been trying that year, and *then* come home and made dinner while his father pouted in the living room with the news. Will had been their only child, and they'd gotten married right out of college, and the whole sexual revolution seemed to have passed his parents right by.

Will sighed and leaned over the table with the blue checked plastic tablecloth and tried not to surmise if it was tree dander or animal dander sticking to the spot in front of him.

"So," his mother said, setting down his iced tea before sitting on the bench across from him.

"So?" He smiled encouragingly—it was his first visit *alone* since their rather surprising phone conversation. Since his mother wouldn't question him about anything personal in front of Aunt Cara, he was expecting a delicate and ladylike filleting from the comfortably middle-aged woman across from him.

"So I guess we can stop trying to fix you up with Cara's assistant after all," his mother teased, and Will grinned until his cheeks popped.

"Aunt Cara already knows," he said, trying to sound serious. "So *that* mission is definitely a no-go."

Anne Lafferty had his same chipmunk-cheeked grin. "Well, *now* it is," she said, rolling her eyes. Suddenly she dropped her voice conspiratorially. "And don't tell *anyone* I said this, but I think Nina sort of has a crush on your aunt Cara anyway."

Will's eyes widened. "Really? *Really?* Really!" He laughed a little, thinking about his last conversation with Cara and her sudden thoughtfulness about whether she should be scoping out Christina Aguilera. Boyfriend after boyfriend had wandered through Cara's life, but they'd all been scared away by her outdoorsy job and her way of calling a fool an asshole and an asshole a waste of fucking skin. And maybe by a reluctance in Cara too. Maybe. "What makes you think that?"

Mom shrugged and drew little pictures in the condensation on her oversize tea glass. "Nothing... just, you know—Nina has this look on her face. Like she's crushing bad."

Will took a sip of his iced tea and tried not to look dubious. And failed. "You can *tell* when someone's doing that?" he asked, feeling suddenly self-conscious.

"I don't know, Will. I could never tell when *you* were doing it!" His mom laughed and relaxed some of her June Cleaver pose, leaning over the table and letting her shoulders drop a little. It was like once she'd dispensed with serving him, she could be his funny, quirky confidante again.

"I never *was* doing it," he confessed. "I never, you know, felt *passionately* about someone before."

His mother put down her iced tea and tilted her head. "But you do now?" she asked, and he shifted uncomfortably.

"Good tea, Mom!" he said brightly and then proceeded to drain his glass so quickly he got brain freeze. While he was going "Ow! Ow! Ow!" his mom brought him the pitcher and a tray of cookies, then sat down and looked at him with such bland interest that he felt like he sort of had to fess up.

"Stop feeding me cookies," he said between mouthfuls of chocolate chip goodness. "I'm trying to lose weight."

"And you look wonderful," she said because she was his mother and she had to. "So, who are you trying to impress?"

He swallowed his cookie and then took a slower, saner drink of tea. "Uhm… Kenny?" he said, wondering how candid she wanted him to be.

His mom reached across the table and took his hand. "You know," she said gently, "I used to be in theater when I was in college."

Will looked around the small backyard of the house in Carmichael. It was mostly grass, with a little concrete apron for the picnic table, and climbing flowers draped all over the little fence. Small, yes, which was why doing one of the few "manly" chores his father used to do wasn't a hardship in the least. It was the place he'd grown up—it felt familiar and cozy, and he didn't worry about being anybody but Will here. It was a comfort that had seen him from the days of wondering if he was just the biggest social abomination known to man to the days of not really giving a crap.

"Theater?" he said, trying to keep his voice casual. In fact, he was *wildly* interested.

"Yes," she said, the corners of her eyes crinkling into one of those truly secretive mom smiles that revealed a whole life their sons knew nothing about. "I wasn't great at the front of the house, but I used to work back of the house. I had fan*tast*ic gaydar. You name a gay man at Sac State, and I had a crush on him."

Will laughed in spite of himself. "Yeah?"

His mom nodded. "Oh yeah. It's one of the reasons I was so crazy about your father. I mean, a great communicator he was *not*, but he *wanted* me. I mean, that's a compliment right there. To be wanted? Not just for your body but for yourself."

Will swallowed and tried really hard not to think about how badly he'd started to want Kenny. "See," he said like he was continuing a conversation, "the thing is, we're friends."

"That's good," his mom said, petting the back of his hand. "The best relationships start as friends."

"Were you and Daddy friends?" he asked baldly.

His mom stopped and thought about it. "We were partners," she said after a pause. "And sometimes that's more important."

"But we're partners too!" Will protested and then blushed. "I mean, Kenny and I. We're doing a project together—you know, sort of a graphic novel thing?"

His mom smiled indulgently, and even though he was pretty sure she didn't get it—fantasy and science fiction had never been her thing—she listened to him babble endlessly about Calandra and Kenny's awesome graphics and how they were going to make their own book. When he was done, his mom nodded and then seemed to file his entire other world in the mental box marked "elsewhere."

"So, friends, partners—does he know you're sort of in love with him?"

Will spit out his iced tea and his mom dissolved into giggles. "It's not funny!" he complained, and she sat back, her hand in front of her mouth, and did her very best to humor him.

"No, of course not," she agreed, but it was hard to hear her through the whoops of laughter.

He cleaned himself off and waited for her to calm down, and then took another drink to hide his embarrassment.

"That wasn't nice," he grumbled, and she nodded—while again hiding her smile behind her hand.

"Which part? The laughing or the bitter truth?"

"How do I know I'm even in love with him?" Will asked seriously. "He's the first gay man I've ever really known."

"But he's not the first *man* you've ever known," his mother said, dabbing at her eyes with a paper napkin and recovering herself. "And he *is* the first man to make you figure out this important thing about yourself. Maybe there's a reason for that."

"But Mom!" Oh God. Twenty-eight years old and whining to his mother. "He's the best friend I've ever had. How do I blow that by telling him he's my first real crush?"

His mom pursed her lips. "Well, honey, like I said. It's nice sometimes just to be wanted. If he's a really good friend, he's not going to hurt you for that."

Will sighed. "It would be *really* good if we could maybe finish our graphic novel first, you think?" he half begged.

His mom gave him one of those little pats on the hand. "Sweetheart, he's *your* relationship. You do what you think is best."

Will swallowed, suddenly realizing that if he was going to ask this, the current mood of gentle candor was the time and place to pitch it. When she was complaining about the Democratic president (he didn't know *why* that was such a big deal) or pissed off at someone at work, she'd say, "William, that's really neither here nor there," and he'd never get a straight answer.

"Mom?"

"What?"

"What would Dad think?"

His mom's shoulders straightened up in an uncomfortable reminder of who she used to be when she was out with his father. Her shoulders were straight and her smile was bright and perfectly proportioned. Will imagined she used to practice that smile in the mirror just to make sure it couldn't be critiqued by his father's business friends and found imperfect.

"Well, sweetheart," she said after a moment, "I don't know if he would have understood. He loved you—of that I have no doubt. But he was always sort of surprised at the amount of raising you required. I swear, he got mad when you were in the first grade because I had to leave work early to get you. He seemed to think that six years old was plenty old enough for you to look after yourself. I had to convince him it would be child abuse—and when he looked it up and saw that yes, I was right, it was child abuse, it was like he'd never seen a real child before, much less been responsible for his welfare."

Will tried to process all of that. "But the gay thing—"

She sighed and stood up. "Here—you grab the pitcher, Will, and I'll take the cookie tray."

"That's a no on the gay?" he asked doggedly, doing what she said because, well, Mom.

She got to the sliding glass door that took them into the back of the house and turned around. "I don't know what to tell you. Five years ago the entire country was sort of rabid on the gay thing, and your dad—he was not an outside-the-box thinker, Will. He didn't have your imagination or the way you have of looking at things and seeing how logical they can be when the rest of the world doesn't understand them." She took a step inside to the darkened interior with the faintly dingy walls. She was always too busy, he thought, to make sure it was all clean all the time. "Your comic book, for instance," she continued as she led the way to the small utilitarian kitchen. "It sounds lovely. But I'm betting your dad would have thought it was some sort of left-wing propaganda because your characters are learning about peace and cooperation. That would have been very him. So, no." She set the cookies down on the countertop and took the pitcher from him to put in the refrigerator. "If you'd have come out in college, it would have been our little secret, yours and mine, and maybe, after you'd met someone and settled down, *then* your dad would have allowed himself to think about it. But that's not what's going to happen with me now."

Okay. That was fair. His mom, who could never be anything *less* than candid, had just given him a simple, painful answer.

He thought about it and decided he had to ask another painful question. "Mom, are you ever going to get married again?"

His mom leaned against the refrigerator and looked at him, obviously choosing her words carefully. She had pulled her hair back from her face with a scrunchie, which was something she'd never done when his father was alive.

"Will, I loved your father—don't get me wrong. But our lives together—there were things he wanted from me that I gave freely, but if I ever found someone again, he'd have to not expect those things from me. I'm never giving them up again. Not for anybody." For a moment her soft, approachable face firmed, became stern and almost fierce, and to his surprise, he understood.

"Sort of like me being straight," he said, because *God*, hadn't he discovered the joy of being himself in the past month. He hadn't needed to kiss anyone or date anyone—just knowing what he *wanted* and that he wanted it *badly*—that was a treat. That right there was ice cream and cookies every damned day.

His mom laughed—and again, it was a sound he didn't remember hearing much when his father was alive. "Yes," she said. "Exactly. Right now, I'm happy and you're gay—and we wouldn't want to change that for the world."

He grinned at her, and they went shopping for plants together, because she enjoyed garden work *much* more than she enjoyed housework, and then they went out for dinner, because nobody insisted she cook to save money, and then he went home.

As he walked into his little apartment and looked around, he thought about Kenny and his pretty house.

They *could* be partners, he thought yearningly. There was so much about them that was right. He just needed to find a way to let Kenny see it.

THAT MONDAY, he texted Kenny to say he'd be by around seven. What he got back made him break into a cold sweat.

Sorry, Will, not tonight. I've got a date.

But—but, a *date*? He had a *date*? But Will hadn't… but, but how could Kenny have a *date* when he was supposed to be property of William Charles Lafferty?

"Well, *maybe* he has a date because he doesn't know you want him like he thinks you want your ex-girlfriend, *dumbass*!"

God. He was so upset he was talking to himself.

Can you go on this date tomorrow?

Okay—if he could go on the date tomorrow, Will could get in his plug (and what a crap choice of words *that* was) for his *own* status of dating Kenny.

Will *really* wanted to date Kenny.

It's just drinks—I'll be home by eight. Maybe you can come by then?

Oh yay oh yay oh yay! Just drinks! That meant probably not just sex! Except what if Kenny decided to have sex in the bathroom *during* drinks? Will had been *reading*, dammit, and he knew very little about gay dating, but he *did* know that lots of people seemed to be having sex in bathrooms, which discouraged the hell out of him because he was six five, 230 pounds of Will-don't-fit-in-a-fuckin'-bathroom!

But still….

Are you going to stop at home to change? I need to talk to you about something.

Okay. His palms were sweaty and he had spots in front of his eyes, but he'd committed. He was going to ask a little question. And he'd made it important.

Yeah—he's picking me up from home. Make it quick?

Okay. It was a window. It was something to work with. He had to phrase that question *really damned well*, but he could do it!

Kenny got home at six. It was almost four. Now Will just had to pick out what he was going to wear.

And what he was going to say.

And how he was going to live with his friend and his broken heart if this did not work out the way he was desperately trying to plan.

HE GOT to Kenny's house about ten minutes early, thinking again as he drove that Kenny's house was the only real bright spot in this neighborhood. A lot of people didn't water their lawns or paint their gutters or plant flowers, but Kenny had done all of the above. His floor plan was a little different than the other houses on the block—his garage extended down, and much of his front lawn had been sacrificed to make a driveway wide enough for a car to turn right into the garage. Kenny made the most out of the space by planting small shrubs in a line instead of having a fence, and by putting blinds with a picture of Mickey Mouse over the window looking into the garage. He'd put a nice bench up on the little concrete apron in front of the house proper, and planted flowers in the beds in front of the apron. The entire house radiated good cheer in a neighborhood where even the private school was too poor to water the grass and there were as many For Sale signs as maintained lawns.

Kenny's house was like a marigold in a mushroom patch, and as Will pulled in, taking the far left space so Kenny could park close to the garage and the front door, he thought miserably that maybe if Kenny *did* go on this date, Will could manage to put his broken heart in his pocket and keep coming over to work on their graphic novel.

He could, right? Like his mom said, he was letting Kenny know he was wanted—it was only fair. Being wanted was a good thing. Since Will was pretty sure he'd never been wanted like that in his whole life, he figured that it must be the most wonderful thing in the world.

He sat nervously in cargo shorts and a button-down shirt, which was sort of a compromise of casual and I-wanna-wear-my-best-courtin'-suit, because it was July in the valley, and 105 degrees was *not* comfortable, even in a button-down. He'd debated getting a gift—wine, flowers, chocolates (ugh, in this heat?)—but he couldn't seem to find a handbook on this. So all he had was himself, his nerves, his clammy hands, and his good intentions.

And his complete befuddlement as a blue Toyota he didn't recognize pulled up into the driveway, taking Kenny's spot. A guy he'd never seen before got out and started opening the garage.

"Hello? Are you Kenny's date for the evening?" Will asked, and the guy startled like he was doing something wrong.

He was tall—a few inches shorter than Will—with blond hair cut shaggy on purpose around a lean face with a square jaw and high cheekbones. He was built rangy, like a baseball player, and wearing *nice* clothes—cargo shorts and a pricey tank top—and up close Will thought he was probably the prettiest man he'd ever seen in his life. As his newly active penis sat up and said howdy-do, his bullshitometer gave it a smack on the cockhead and screamed, "Asshole alert! Asshole alert! Do *not* trust that cheesy smile, come-for-brains. This man is *not* your friend!"

"Hey—no, I'm not Kenny's date, I'm his *boyfriend*. What? Are you neighborhood watch or something?"

Will scowled and stood up, pulling out his phone. Okay, yeah. Now the guy looked a little familiar—and so did the car—but Will had forgotten he'd ever seen either one of them before. "So you're Gifford?" he asked pleasantly, not answering the question. "Does Kenny know you're getting into his garage?"

Gif's smile didn't move, but his eyes narrowed. "Well, the ex thing is really only temporary," he said smoothly, and Will narrowed his eyes in return as he tapped urgently on his phone.

Your ex is here getting into your garage. Lethal force?

He took a few steps toward Gif with his stomach in and his shoulders squared and for once in his life didn't try to make himself five ten. "Now, I happen to know that's a load of bullshit," he said pleasantly. "A guy doesn't take two HIV tests because he broke up with someone 'temporarily,' so maybe you could back away from his garage until he gets here."

"Who in the hell *are* you?" Gif rolled his eyes in clear dismissal. "Well, whoever the hell you are, you don't know Kenny very well. He's *never* home before eight!"

"He has been, to work with me," Will said evenly. "And he *is* coming home *now*, so maybe whatever you're taking out of his garage can wait until he gets here."

Will's phone buzzed angrily, and he didn't have to see Kenny's startled *FUCK!* to know that sleazoid ex-boyfriend was up to no good.

"So just out of curiosity," Will said, taking a few bold steps closer, "what were you planning to steal? Just so we know who to ask when it comes up missing?"

Gif laughed like Will was cracking a joke, and made a go at brazening it out. "I left my bike here when I moved out." He smiled disarmingly. "I just thought I'd come by when it wasn't a big deal and get—"

"The twenty-inch frame that would be ridiculously small on you?" Will said, crossing his arms. "Because you, you'd be okay on a twenty-two inch, but you'd probably want a twenty-three inch like I've got." He'd been riding it a *lot* lately since gas was so expensive and he was so partially employed.

Gif's smile finally dimmed like it suddenly occurred to him that he wasn't going to bullshit his way through this. "Look, man, I don't want a big hassle, I was just coming for my bike—"

"Which isn't here," Will said stonily. And hey, hello, there was Kenny, parking behind Will, and Will thanked God because it meant this guy could finally leave.

"Jesus," Kenny snapped as he got out of his smart car. "Are you really trying to steal my stuff?"

"It's not stealing when it's yours!" Gif snarled, grabbing the handle so he could throw the garage door open. Will shoved his hand down, catching the handle on his palm and sending the door smashing to the ground—and right on top of Gif's sandal-shod foot!

"Ow-ow-ow-ow!" Gif hopped backward and leaned against his car, cradling his foot and looking damned ridiculous. "Jesus, Gigantor, could you *be* any clumsier?" He scowled up at Will and Will scowled back.

"You *so* earned that," Kenny snapped. "Now get in your car and drive away before I call the police and produce the damned receipt for whatever is in that house that you think you own."

"Your bike," Will said, folding his arms and making a human blockade of himself in front of Kenny's garage.

Kenny gave his ex-boyfriend a look of pure, undiluted loathing. "You were going to pawn my bicycle? That was a gift from my *parents*!"

"And thus, the only thing in the house without a receipt," Will supplied, and Gif turned all his venom on Will.

"Who in the fuck *are* you!"

"I'm the guy you have to go through to hurt Kenny *ever again*. Now go. Away."

Gif scowled at Kenny. "I hope he's hung like a frickin' donkey, Kenny, because he's not much to look at!"

And Kenny slapped him across the face.

Will winced. He'd actually been in a couple of fistfights as a kid—he remembered his father telling him how to hold his hand so he didn't hurt his thumb. When he saw Kenny's hand lift, he was expecting a full-out punch. The slap, though—that was just demeaning.

What was even more demeaning was Gif's self-satisfied smile. "He must be more butch than he looks if you're gonna bitch slap me over him," he gloated, and *that's* when Will tried to plow his fist through Gifford Boyle's eye. They were standing pretty close, though, and Gif's car was at his back, so he went stumbling back into his car, bounced off, and landed on his hands and knees.

Gif howled and collapsed, holding his hands over his eye, and Will shook out his hand and hissed. "Damn! Everything from my knuckles to my shoulder! What is he made out of, concrete?"

"You hit him!" Kenny protested, and Will tried not to whine like a complete loser.

"Not a good idea," he muttered. He toed Gif in the side a little. "If we get you some ice, will you go away?" he shouted like he was talking to a deaf old grandmother.

"No! Ow-ow-ow-ow—I'm gonna press charges!"

"And tell them what?" Will demanded, prodding him with his flip-flop again. "That you tried to steal your ex-boyfriend's bicycle?"

"Augh!" Gif shouted. "Go-the-fuck-away!"

And then, to complete the merriment and turn the whole can of worms into a bucket of snakes, another car pulled up.

"Oh fuck," Kenny said, his voice taking on that dreamy quality of someone who feels like he's in way above his head. "There's Cliff. He's early."

Will's adrenaline was still up, and he glowered at the trim guy jumping out of the teal-blue Hyundai like *he* was responsible for all that was wrong in Will's life.

"Cliff the date?" he asked, his growliness not going away.

"Yes, Cliff the date—"

"Gifford and Clifford—Jesus, Kenny, were you going for bookends? A gift set? Can you not date losers for just a fucking nanosecond?"

"I don't know he's a loser! What's wrong with you?" Kenny slapped ineffectually at Will's bicep, and Will grabbed his hand.

"Could you not go out with Cliff the date tonight?" Will said, all of his carefully rehearsed awkward words burned away by the stupid ex-boyfriend and the fact that Will had actually *hit* someone, leveled him, and he was still writhing on the ground.

Kenny grunted. "Here, Will, help me get him in the car." Kenny bent over, tugging on Gif's arm, and Will sighed.

"Move over," he muttered. "I'll get him." He bent at the knees, because he *did* work out, and grabbed Gif under the arms and then straightened up, bearing all the weight in his thighs.

"Jesus God, you are fucking strong," Kenny said, eyes big, and Will grunted.

"Open his door, would you?"

Fortunately, Gif had left the door unlocked, so Will could drag him around the car and drop his sorry ass in the seat. After the first couple of steps, Will realized that the asshole was fully capable of walking all on his own, but he was making himself limp so he could whine more.

"I will drop you," he snarled. "I will drop you and you will bruise your ass, and we will leave you lying on the concrete."

Gif straightened up and Will changed his grip so he could *steer* the guy into the car.

"If you come back again, I will kick your ribs into your heart," Will threatened. Given that he'd seen Kenny *draw* that scene in their graphic novel, he was pretty sure it could be done.

Gif groaned and leaned his forehead against the steering wheel. "Fine. Fucking fine." He sat up and screamed, trying to get in one last shot. "See if I come back, bottom boy! You're going to be *screaming* for a guy with an IQ over sixty-five!"

"Cliff!" Kenny called, and the guy who'd gotten out of the car paused as Kenny held up a hand. "Hold on a minute." He turned to Gif and said, "Will's brilliant—he makes you look functionally brain damaged. Now go."

Will made sure Gif was clear from the door before slamming it, and then he turned to Kenny and, out of desperation, grabbed both his shoulders and turned him.

"Here, are you focused?" he asked, and Kenny glared over his shoulder as Gif turned the ignition and started to back out. Will gave him a little shake and said it again. "Are. You. Focused?"

Kenny shook his head and stared at him. "Will, did you really just beat up my ex-boyfriend?"

"Did you really make a date for tonight?"

Kenny waved at Cliff over his shoulder. "Yes, so?"

"Tell him you can't go!"

"What? Why?"

"Because—"

Will felt a tap on his shoulder, and he completely lost his patience with a total stranger. "*What?*" he yelled, and Cliff took a step back.

"Kenny, are you okay? He's not threatening you, is he?"

Kenny was staring at Will like he'd lost his mind, and he shook himself and answered his date. "No—*no*. Cliff, he's fine. He's the world's nicest guy, he was just helping me out of a jam."

"He looks like he's bullying you," Cliff said, and he took a step toward Will like he was going to be a big man. "I don't like bullies—who are you and what are you doing here?"

And *God*, Will was tired of being asked that.

"*I'm* the guy who's been crushing on Kenny for a month, asshole, and I'm here to ask him to give me a fucking chance!"

Cliff squinted at Kenny. "I thought you said you were single?"

And Kenny—oh, the look on his face was not good. "Cliff, could we do this another night?" he asked, and Cliff held up a hand and rolled his eyes.

"Whatever, princess—you know my number." And he was forgotten before they even heard the slam of his door.

"Will, you can't say things like that," Kenny said. His face was pale, his lips white, everything about him cold and bloodless.

"But—but I *want* you," Will said, remembering what his mom had told him. "I want you—isn't that a good thing? Even if you don't want me back, don't you like knowing that I want you?"

Kenny hauled both hands through his short hair and tried to back up, but Will wouldn't let him. "I liked knowing you were dependable, that's what I liked knowing. God! You can't want me! You can't! You're not—"

"Gay? But I *am!*" Will's hands were still on Kenny's shoulders, and he softened his grip. "You taught me that—you told me what to look for, and the only person I can see after that is you!"

Kenny broke away from him and wiped his eyes with the back of his hand. "But don't you get it? If we were friends, then that would be us for life! But if you want me, you'll just drop me. I'm all shiny and pretty now because I'm the first gay man you saw, but the shiny will wear off, and I'll just be the slutty guy who first slept with you, and you won't even want to come work on the project or—"

He was crying. Oh God. Kenny was *crying*. And Will wanted to make it better.

Will pulled him into his arms and enfolded him, wrapping Kenny's smaller body into his chest and his arms and just holding him, waiting for the shaking to stop.

"I swear," he said, stooping slightly so he could kiss the top of Kenny's head. "I swear, I want you because you're my friend, not because you're pretty. You'd think that, I know, but I keep looking at other guys and expecting to feel the same thing, and some of them are pretty, but you just keep getting… shinier. Better."

Kenny was struggling out of his arms, and that wouldn't do at all. Will had just gotten used to him being there. "No—don't you get it? I'm like your gaypiphany—that's not a lasting thing, Will, that's—"

Will kissed him.

Mouth over mouth, until whatever Kenny was trying to say faded into a whimper, and Will groaned in the back of his throat, because oh my God, *this* was kissing. *This* was someone's taste—harsh and sweet with soda and cinnamon gum. *This* was why they made such a big deal of it in the movies. Kenny moaned back, the sound resonating in Will's mouth, and Will thrust his tongue forward and tasted and tasted and tasted.

Kenny went soft in his arms, yielding, pliant. He wrapped his arms around Will's neck, and Will cupped his taut, perky little bottom and lifted. Kenny took the hint, wrapping his legs around Will's waist, and Will carried him, a step at a time, toward the house.

He got to the entryway and stopped walking, leaning Kenny against the wall so he could set him down.

"Mmmnnn…." Kenny refused to end the kiss and refused to put his feet down, and Will grimaced, thinking he wasn't *that* strong.

"Key," he gasped before taking another kiss. "Key! Inside!"

Kenny pulled back—but kept his legs wrapped around Will's hips. "I am *not* having sex with you!" he gasped.

"I don't even know what that means," Will mumbled and kissed him some more. Pure water after a desert thirst had nothing on Kenny Scalia after a lifetime dry spell. Kenny's legs clasped tighter and omigod there was a bulge in his pants and it ground up against Will's bulge and it was *heavenly* but not enough. "Keys, Kenny!"

Kenny's response was to hold Will's face in place so he could plunder Will's mouth this time. Will opened, hungry, wanting. *It's nice to be wanted.* God, Kenny *wanted* him.

Kenny's feet touched the ground and he pulled Will down to him. Will let himself be pulled, and Kenny ate him alive.

Will dug in the pockets of Kenny's chinos for his goddamned keys. Oops, got a little personal there—

"Gahh!" Kenny panted, twisting his hips and thrusting towards Will's palm. "Will, please—"

Will found the godforsaken keys. His hand shook as he fumbled with the lock, and Kenny whimpered and ground against his thigh. They crashed through the door, and Will remembered to slam it shut behind them so Princess didn't get out. Will pushed Kenny up against the closed door, kissing his neck, shoving his mustard-yellow polo shirt up and mauling that tight, compact little body while Kenny made keening little moans over his head.

"Will, this—talk, we need to—"

Will found an absurdly small plum-colored nipple and pulled it into his mouth, playing the end with his tongue.

Kenny whined and clenched his hands in Will's hair, so Will felt free to continue. He kissed and suckled tender ribs and a skin-soft abdomen while Kenny leaned back against the door and closed his eyes, and Will had no doubts where he was heading. He straightened a little for Kenny's other nipple while he worked Kenny's belt, and then Kenny's clothes seemed to dissolve, giving Will free access to all points south.

He sank to his knees and kissed down a dark-furred happy trail, pausing a few inches below Kenny's tiny divot of a navel to look up.

Kenny was looking down at him, stroking Will's hair, his forehead, his cheeks. "I want to do this *so* badly," Will confessed with a little smile, and Kenny nodded, closing his eyes.

"I don't want to stop you."

Will grinned then, full-out. "That is *excellent* news!"

He licked down to the thick black pubic hair and then stopped and nuzzled it, because the strands were silky and because it *smelled* so different than a woman did, and the smell was dark and sharp and rich and he loved it.

Kenny's hands tugged reassuringly in his hair, and he looked up and smiled wickedly, then ran his tongue from the root, right where the hair ended, very slowly to the tip. He got to the end and started to play, licking broadly across the head, teasing the slit, diddling with the little guitar string of the frenulum, until Kenny let out a long, frustrated moan.

"Will, precious? I hate to rush you here, but...."

Will engulfed Kenny's crown before letting his evil chuckle rumble around his palate, promptly rewarded with a little spatter of precome. He flattened his tongue against Kenny's cock and decided it didn't taste that bad, and then pushed his head further, making sure he covered his teeth—and wrapped his tongue around the shaft as much as humanly possible.

The sound Kenny let out was more than encouragement, it was a *reward*.

Will pulled back, sucking hard, and then let the suction pull him forward. Kenny's cockhead was a little uncomfortable in the back of his throat, but Kenny made that growl/moan/hiccup sound again, and Will wanted it—wanted *him*—more. *Anything*, he thought, stroking back and forth again. *Anything*—shoving his head forward and swallowing just to have more of Kenny inside him.

"Will!" Kenny protested. "Will, I'm going to come!"

So? HIV-free—Will knew it for a fact. Kenny could come and come and come and Will could make him, and that was just amazing!

"*Will!*"

Will swallowed him deeper, then pulled back and wrapped his hand around and stroked firmly toward the crown, opening his mouth when his fist got to the end.

Kenny's entire body spasmed, and Will wrapped his other hand around Kenny's hip to ground him. The cock in Will's hand spat come, irregular white clots, and Will closed his eyes, opened his mouth, and let it happen.

"Nngn," Kenny groaned, and tightened his hand in Will's hair to the point of pain and then let go. Will felt both hands on his face, wiping come from under his eyes, and when his eyes were clear, he opened them and smiled sunnily up at Kenny.

Who was looking dazedly back at him. "Proud of yourself?" he asked rhetorically.

Will bobbed his head enthusiastically. "Absolutely," he said and then grimaced. He was a big guy—being on the floor on his knees was *not* comfortable.

"Want some help up?" Kenny asked, nodding because they both knew it was true.

"Yes, please," he asked, not humbly at all. Kenny reached down and helped lever him to his feet, and before he could say anything else, Will wiped his face off on the sleeve of his shirt and kissed him.

This was a different kiss—tender, sweet—and when he pulled back for air, his chest still felt full of sunshine. Kenny's answering smile didn't do anything to bring the clouds.

"You want me," Kenny said softly.

"More than anything in the world," Will told him sincerely.

"Ready to see what all of me is like?" There was something fragile about Kenny in that moment, and Will wondered how many Giffords, how many Cliffs, had breezed through his life.

"If you can stand to see all of me," he answered back, looking Kenny straight in those dark-blue eyes.

Kenny's lower lip trembled. "I've wanted you for so long," he said, his voice shaking, and Will didn't want any sadness, not tonight.

This kiss was warm and full, and Will wrapped his arms around Kenny's waist and lifted him clean out of his loafers, chinos, and boxer shorts.

And then carried him to the magic bedroom, the one place in the house he'd never been.

The bed was king-size, the furniture was simple oak, and the bedspread was the same color as Kenny's eyes.

"AW!" NINA crowed, clapping her hands. "That story was *amazing*! Thanks so much for telling it!"

"And now let's dance!" Cara said gruffly, standing up and tugging on her bride's hand. They disappeared into the throng, and Will took Kenny's hand.

"Want to dance?" Kenny asked hopefully, and Will shrugged, trying not to feel self-conscious.

"I'm still not very coordinated—"

Kenny cut him off with a roll of his eyes. "It's pretty packed out there. C'mon, big man—they're playing 'Open Arms.' All you have to do is hold me and dance...." He faltered, because they both remembered those words, and their eyes met as something warm and tender passed between them.

"Sure," Will said, standing and letting himself be towed to the dance floor. Once they got there, Will folded in his arms in a perfect tuck, and Kenny nestled in there like he was hiding from hurt.

He'd grown melancholy as Will was telling his part of the story, and Will sort of thought he knew the problem, but he wasn't always sure.

"Do you think they know?" Kenny mumbled into his chest.

"That we stopped before the end of the story?" Will asked, kissing the top of his head and smiling.

"Yeah—I mean, it sounded like the happy ever after, but there's more."

"Well, yeah!" Will pulled back enough to kiss him softly on the lips this time. "I want there to be a lot more. There should *always* be more. The story should go happy ever after 'til death do us part!'"

Kenny wrinkled his nose, and Will could tell he was trying to look annoyed. "God, don't be morbid." His mock annoyance faded. "Will it really?"

Will shifted his stance and murmured into Kenny's ear. "Do *you* remember what happened after that?"

Kenny's smile up at him was, in Kenny's own words, precious. "All of it, right up until this moment."

Will smiled back, and he was pretty sure it was that same half-embarrassed, half-wicked, all-infatuated grin Kenny was giving him.

"Me too," he said, under the music and the babble of couples dancing.

"It's only been nine months," Kenny said primly, and Will laughed.

"Yeah, but you're even shinier now."

"Yeah?" And oh, there went that wistful quality to his voice. If Will could do anything, he would take that away. He would make Kenny believe he would always be bright and glittery, like bubbles in a crystal decanter of champagne.

"Yeah." Will nodded. God. He wondered if Kenny remembered the past nine months with as much joy as he did. "It's been the best year of my life."

"Mine too," Kenny confessed to Will's shirtfront, and Will grinned.

"Honest?"

"That night was like… like… perfect."

Excellent. Kenny must be remembering it just like Will was. At least Will hoped so.

PRETTY PLATES
AND OTHER DAZZLING THINGS

WILL'S BODY was even better than Kenny had imagined.

Yeah, part of that was that he'd been riding his bike and working out a lot in the past six weeks, but most of it?

Was just… solid. He wasn't fat so much as solid. His chest, his arms, his thighs, even his knotty calves, were substantial. He'd lifted Kenny like a kid and kissed him all the way into the bedroom, and Kenny had *trusted* that. How often in his dating life had Kenny trusted anything? His parents, bless them, had raised him, pampered him, and sent him to art school, and he'd taken the freedom of college and pretty much fucked his way into a productive adulthood.

But never, not in a boyfriend's bed or a stranger's arms, had he had that security he'd felt as a kid, sleeping in his own bed, with his brother down the hall. Not since he'd taken his first plane to San Diego and his parents had proudly proclaimed he was an adult. That was why the house—even if he could only afford one in a crappy neighborhood. That was why he kept trying to make it pretty, even when Gif had lived there and hadn't appreciated it.

Will appreciated it. *Will* loved home, and loved solid, and loved real.

Will was standing in his bedroom, having just taken off his shirt, and was peeping out at Kenny from under his brows, hoping Kenny found him acceptable.

No spit, no breath, no words. Kenny stepped into Will's space, placing a careful hand on Will's bicep. He squeezed a little, remembering that first night and how he could not stop groping the straight boy.

He swallowed hard and flattened his palm along Will's triceps, aware his lips were slightly parted and his heart was thundering in his throat.

"You look so serious," Will rumbled, and Kenny looked up into that dear face. Not handsome, no, and even leaner it was still a very stolid square, but God. The more Kenny knew of him, the more roots he put down in Kenny's heart, the more beautiful he appeared.

"You are a very serious lover," Kenny said, clearing his throat twice to get it out. "You... when you leave, it's going to take me more than fifteen minutes to find someone else."

Will stretched out a gentle fingertip and traced it across Kenny's cheekbone, ending with a tap on the nose that made Kenny look up and meet his eyes. "I'll have to make sure I never leave," he said seriously. "Eat my veggies, drive safe, only go out for a beer if you're going to take me home."

Kenny laughed a little and blinked hard. "I will *always* take you home," he whispered, and Will framed his face with both hands and kissed him again.

Kenny made sure to take advantage of the kiss, rubbing his exposed chest against Will's and planing his hands across every muscle, every ripple on his arms and his back. For his part, Will finished with the buttons on Kenny's shirt and slid it down his shoulders, and now they were both skin on skin, naked and panting. Kenny slid a hand down between them and....

"Oh holy God," he muttered, grasping Will's cock and realizing that his finger and thumb didn't touch. "You were *not* kidding!" His glare at Will was faintly accusatory, because... oh my *God*!

He could see the blush travelling under the fair skin below Will's neck and above the middle of his arms. It hit his throat first and then spread in patches across his chest and abdomen. Kenny started kissing the edges of the pink blotches, and the hiss of Will's breath told him he was doing okay.

"Gif's skinnier," Will said, and Kenny suckled on a tan nipple until he heard a satisfying grunt. He released Will's flesh, and oh, it was tasty, salty, sweet, and Will.

"Gif's not here," Kenny mumbled against the dividing line between his pecs. "Will's here, and he's better company."

"Oh wow, that's better than I imagined," Will breathed, and Kenny went to sink to his knees, but Will stopped him. "On the bed," he said, nodding.

Kenny smirked at him a little. "For a guy who's never done this before, you're awfully bossy."

Will shook his head. "I've had sex before," he insisted. "It may have been girls, but that's what made it sex. It was hands and mouths and… and *things*, but it wasn't the right person."

Kenny had to close his eyes. "Me too," he said, and they both knew he wasn't talking about girls.

"It's the right person," Will said softly, seriously.

"Me too." And oh, it was. This guy wasn't anyone to mess with. This wasn't a quick fuck with a lingering relationship. This was the first guy since he was twelve years old and came out (and came on to) his ex-best friend who gave a shit about what Kenny Scalia said, or how he thought, or what sort of drawings he did.

This was the first guy in his life who ever *got* Kenny in a way that made Kenny happy just to sit next to him on the couch.

They were standing so close, Kenny could feel the heat from Will's body, the faint sheen of sweat from the time he'd spent outside, and every breath he took brought Will's chest just close enough to brush the few silky black hairs on Kenny's. Will cupped his chin, and suddenly Kenny was face to face with the most important man in his life since his father.

"So it's not like sex," Will said, that sweet smile on his face. "It's like dancing. If you want it to be special, all you have to do is hold me and dance."

And with that, Will wrapped his arms around Kenny's waist, bending down a little to make fit. Kenny placed his hands on Will's shoulders, and they rubbed together, skin to skin, and kissed, made out naked, standing in Kenny's room, until Kenny's entire body sang and he needed so many things at once he was breathless with it.

"Lie down," he panted. "Lie down, and I want to—" He clenched his fingers against the hard muscles of Will's pecs. "God, I've wanted to grope your chest since we *met*," he complained. "Can I just *touch* you?"

And like that, the awkwardness was gone, and the "who bossed who around" part too. Without breaking contact, Kenny pulled the cover back and then scrambled into bed, fully aware that Will was right behind him.

The sheets were cool and clean against his skin, and Kenny held out his arms until Will could get comfortable again. They kissed and kissed until it got frantic, and more passionate, and the touch of Will's body just *fed* Kenny, made his cock hard, made his groin throb with every skate of lips or hands or skin against skin. Kenny scooted close enough to grind against Will, craving the touch of their flesh together, and Will dropped his hand between them and grasped both of their cocks.

Of course he did that, Kenny thought deliriously. Of course he did. Kenny wouldn't have been able to fit both their members in one of his hands, but Will could do it. Kenny arched his back, driving his cock in Will's grip, and Will squeezed a little tighter. Both of them were drooling precome, and when the fluid, hot and slippery, hit Kenny's cockhead, he groaned into Will's mouth.

Oh, this was not what he'd had in mind. He wanted to taste Will, wanted to suck him so good, wanted to grease himself up and sit on that fat prick and make them both scream—

The images ran through his mind, making him hotter, but nothing could have pulled him away from this frantic, grasping, clutching frottage that Gif would have laughed at but Kenny didn't ever want to end.

Will's groan—low, sexy, totally helpless—was Kenny's only warning, and he wrenched himself out of Will's grasp to get his head in position to take Will's cock in his mouth as Will jacked himself off. Oh God, it was bigger, and tastier, and just… just *Will*. It was all the things he'd dreamed of when yearning for Will, but better and more fulfilling, because it was really him.

Will groaned, and his come spewed sweet and bitter and salty— Kenny knew this taste, but it had never been this good. He swallowed, because he'd practiced, but even more, because it was an offering.

No man had ever done this with William Lafferty before. No man had ever sucked that thing into the back of his throat and swallowed. No man had ever seen the parts of Will that Kenny had just memorized by touch, and Kenny—who had never given a rat's ass where his partners had been as long as they wore a rubber when they got to Kenny—was suddenly possessive of that.

Will was his. Of all the people who could have hit Kenny's garbage can, Kenny got funny, kind Will Lafferty, and he was going to suck, lick, bite, and hickeyfy whatever parts of that tan-and-white body he needed to in order to keep this man in his bed.

The thought made him come just from rutting against the bedsheet, and even as the stars exploded behind his own eyes, he didn't stop sucking Will's cock.

Will groaned and started to shake, because everything in Kenny's mouth was now tender, thoroughly used and made clean by Kenny, who was reluctant to ever let it go.

He did, though, and pulled up to kiss Will, come still riming his lips like salt on a margarita glass. Will apparently didn't care. He kissed Kenny, plundered his mouth, and tasted his own seed, grunting in satisfaction. Their breath eased before they gave up the kiss, and Kenny wiped his mouth on the sheets before smiling.

"Hold each other and dance, huh?"

Will smiled dazedly. "Well, maybe we should save dancing like that for private," he breathed, and Kenny nodded with enthusiasm.

"My thoughts *exactly*."

They kissed again, in communication, but as they pulled away, Kenny knew the sex was still waiting, but now the communication mattered.

He pulled back from the kiss and felt Will's fingertips tickling the curve of his neck to his shoulder.

"What?" Kenny smiled, and Will stroked it again.

"Is it stupid, that it's all magic to me?"

Kenny shook his head. "No," he whispered. Surprisingly, their next kiss generated some heat, and the next, and the next, because touching Will without heat, without tenderness, without *heart,* turned out to be something Kenny absolutely could not do.

THEY NEVER did "do the thing"—the scary thing that so attracted and horrified Will after dumping over the trash can. They had, instead, kissed and frotted and sucked and stroked just like new lovers, like teenagers, still exploring. Eventually they stopped and showered, and Kenny fed them something simple.

It had to be simple—Will was still in his boxers and his T-shirt, and Kenny was still in his boxers, and neither of them were dressed to either cook or eat a gourmet meal.

So they ate Asian noodles over the sink and talked softly, never separating far enough that touch was out of the question.

"How long have you known?" Kenny asked, making sure his mouth was full so Will couldn't hear his hurt.

"The day after we met," Will said, his own mouth full—probably just from hunger. "You gave me that book—turned out to be a good investment. I'd never really looked at porn before. Would you believe it? Cocks make me hard and those other parts don't?"

Will's (full) mouth quirked up, inviting Kenny in on the joke, but he couldn't feel it.

"But you never *said* anything," he wailed, feeling absurdly left out.

Will sighed and swallowed the rest of his mouthful. "I know. And I'm sorry. But I didn't want to do what you just thought I was doing— imprint on the first gay man to ever answer my questions. So, you know, I stroked off a lot on my own time, and you and I got to be friends, and the more I was around you, the more I knew—"

"Knew what?" Kenny said, hungry for the words again, even if Will had already said them.

Will set his mostly empty bowl down and moved into Kenny's body, framing his hips with those big hands of his. "I knew that yeah, I was gay, and yeah, I was attracted to men. But what I felt for *you* wasn't just attraction, it was the whole nine yards. It was attraction and friendship and partnership and...."

He trailed off and blushed, and Kenny thought that maybe it was too early for either of them to say it, even if that was what they were thinking. Too many new things to talk about, too many new things to do. So they finished their noodles and went back to the bedroom and did some more of those new things, and then they lay naked and replete in Kenny's bed and watched something stupid on television like they were an old married couple, and the old married things made them just as happy too.

Kenny wondered, as he closed his eyes and snuggled backward into Will's body, how long this would last.

THE FIRST month was sort of delirious. It just... it was *so perfect*.

Will worked on his web-design business while Kenny was at work, and by the time Kenny got home, Will would be waiting. Kenny would greet him at the door with a kiss. Then they'd put Will's bike in the garage and proceed to talk about their days as they got dinner ready. Sometimes Will brought takeout, and sometimes he brought ingredients, and sometimes Kenny had something planned, but the food was incidental. It was the conversation that was the crux of the thing, and afterward, it was the highly satisfying work they did together on their graphic novel.

When they'd worked long enough, they'd stand and stretch, and... and Kenny didn't even remember who started it most of the time. It would be Will brushing the back of his neck with thick, fluttery fingers, or Kenny reaching out to slide a hand down Will's hip. And then there would be kissing, glorious kissing, scads and scads of kissing, until they had kissed each other naked and were rolling around on the bed, kissing and sucking and coming.

It was *awesome*, but that didn't mean Kenny didn't want to get Will to try that other thing too. Kenny had been reamed too many times—and loved it—to think full-bore penetration should be something to give up because Will was plug shy.

So one day, while squirming in his cubicle, thinking of the many things he and Will had yet to teach each other about their bodies, he pulled out his phone.

I'm going to be a little late tonight. Gotta make a stop.

He waited a moment and then added, *And bring the stuff in the little striped bag.*

What he got back was *???*

You heard me! We're gonna do some experimentation. We need tools and lubricant, just like working on a car.

There was a pause.

Do you want a banana in your tailpipe?

And because he was Will, and he didn't pout, and he was as excited as a puppy to learn new things, Kenny could answer him truthfully.

God, yes. Please.

Your kink is my command.

Oh Jesus, he loved this guy. He really, *really* loved this guy!

I love you so much.

!!!!!!!!!!!!

Oh fuck. He'd said that. He hadn't just said that, he'd *texted* it, and there it would sit, for posterity, to mock him. Kenny hadn't learned when he walked in on his boyfriend boning another guy, because he'd fallen for the next straight guy who came along, and here he was, teaching the straight guy how to be gay, and he'd fallen for him like an idio—

Stop freaking out. I love you too. I would especially love to say that in person.

Kenny looked at the text in surprise, and his heartbeat roared to a hush in his ears.

Me too.

Oh God. He'd confirmed it. He trusted. It was a shock, even to *him.* He trusted. He trusted Will to say it to him, face to face. It was a miracle, that's what it was. A frickin' miracle, and he was going to try to fuck that up with sexual playtime?

Good. Will bring striped bag. You get something big and yummy for yourself.

He startled, looking at the text.

Well, maybe he wasn't going to fuck anything up. Maybe, when the relationship was good and the partner was solid, maybe that was what sex *didn't* do. Maybe if you were doing it right, sex just made it stronger.

"You okay?"

Cam's voice almost shocked him out of his bemused, happy little trance.

"Yeah," he said with a little smile. "Just, you know… doing the dance with the significant other." Maybe he should actually say "boyfriend." It wasn't like Cam had ever said anything actively homophobic.

"Well, yeah—that shit's important," Cam said, nodding seriously. "Take ten—you work too goddamned hard."

Kenny brought him a Dr Pepper at least twice a week, and for his part, when Cam brought his buddies muffins on Friday, he made sure Kenny got one. Kenny hadn't even *known* Cam did that until this past month.

Kenny smiled at him now. "Well, you know. Maybe it's time to play a little." He raised his eyebrows and Cam lifted his soda in toast.

"Amen!" he said.

Kenny squirmed in his seat and thought about Will and the little striped bag.

"A*men*."

HE'D GIVEN Will his own key the week before, so he wasn't surprised to get home and see that there was a spinach, tomato, and cheese casserole in the oven with an hour to go, and that the table was already set for two. Will seemed to enjoy these details as much as Kenny did, and Kenny always brightened when he walked in the door and found, hello, his life really did fit at a table set for two.

But Will wasn't in the kitchen, and he wasn't in the living room, and Kenny walked back to the bedroom, striped plastic bag clutched in his hand, trying to still the nasty little shudder in the pit of his stomach, because the last time he'd done something like this, the results had been less than stellar.

But he got to the bedroom and there was no Will naked and cavorting with some other guy. Instead, there was a tiger-striped bag on the still-made bed. He set his bag down next to that one and turned to find his Will coming out of the bedroom shower, fresh scrubbed and sweet smelling and smiling shyly.

"What?" Kenny asked, surprised at that shy smile. "I mean hi, and what?"

Will looked anywhere but at him. "I, uhm, you know. Read up. Uhm. Prepped. Uhm. Stuff. So we can… whatever."

Kenny's smile took over his whole body. "Okay," he said, walking into Will's space and toying with the edge of the towel wrapped around his waist. "I'll, uhm, go get all… sweet too."

Will breathed in like that touch at his middle excited him. "What should I do?"

Kenny kissed his temple. "You look at the book, find all your favorite parts, and look and look and don't touch yourself."

Will grinned and shivered. "You're not gonna know what hit you."

"I already don't know," Kenny confessed. "But it makes me *really* happy."

He got out of the shower and there Will was, naked in his bed, studying that big ol' book of porn like a kid studying a math book. The only thing different—besides the big adult body—was the fully erect cock lying on Will's abdomen, glistening with precome. Kenny shuddered and remembered to bring a clean cloth with him, partially damped down, as well as a towel to put over the sheets. He pulled the comforter down all the way, stretched out the towel, and then started rooting around in the bags.

For a moment, all he could hear was the rattle of the thick plastic bags and the packaging around the plain black butt plug and Will's heated breathing. Kenny set the bag on the end table and started lubing the plug, and he looked up to see Will had stopped studying the porn and was now studying him.

"What's the plan?" he asked.

Kenny, who had met his last boyfriend being fucked in a club bathroom, flushed with gratification. He trusted Will—he wasn't going to find this man screwing around on him because he was bored. Will was *mesmerized* by him. And Will trusted him.

It warmed his stomach and tied it in knots at the same time.

"See," Kenny said, blushing, "I'm going to… well, we're going to use this in you, and you're going to feel me getting you all ready, and you're going to feel how good it is, right?"

Will nodded excitedly, and Kenny bit his lip, hoping that this would work. "And then, I figure, you do the same thing for me except, you know, not a plug, right?"

Will's grin stretched his cheeks. "Do I get to swear? Can we say *fuck*, Kenny? 'Cause *fuck*!"

Kenny shivered from the top of his head to the ends of his toes. "I knew you could," he whispered in praise.

And then he couldn't talk about it anymore. He rolled over to his side and started kissing Will's outer thigh, hair and all, and then moved his kisses to Will's abdomen, and then—yes, *yes*—his erect cock.

Will sighed and shuddered, relaxing into the feel of Kenny's mouth as Kenny relaxed into his taste. This was his man, warm and bitter, and Kenny rolled over his leg and into the V of his thighs, confident that Will would lift his knees and spread his thighs, because Will craved his touch as much as Kenny craved Will's.

Will opened for him, and Kenny tasted, stroked, sucked, and fondled until the stream of precome drizzled almost nonstop. (Will did this, and it was both comforting and amazingly sexy—Kenny had never felt more wanted in his life than when he had to change sheets once a night.)

Then, when Will was moaning, thrusting up mindlessly, relaxed enough to know when Kenny would back off if he couldn't take it, Kenny stroked his finger down Will's crease.

He expected Will to clench, to tighten and maybe to reject that touch outright, but Will must have been studying porn more than

Kenny thought, because he spread his knees wider, and that comforting drizzle of precome never stopped.

Kenny rubbed his finger around Will's rim, softening him up, loosening him, and when it was time to slip his finger in, Will moaned at the same time he pushed against the little invader, and it slipped right in.

"Oooh," Will said, and Kenny *hmm*ed and kissed the side of Will's thigh.

"Good?" Kenny asked.

"Great," Will breathed. "Keep going!"

Kenny used two fingers next, stretching subtly and deep and making sure he hit Will's gland enough to make Will shudder. He took that moment to engulf Will's prick again, slurping on it hard, and then he wiggled himself against the sheets.

He was hard and leaking too, just from making Will ready.

Very carefully, he slipped his two fingers out, gratified by Will's little keen of reluctance. Also very carefully, he gently pushed the plug in, and Will's full-throated groan of acceptance almost made him come.

Will started shifting his hips restlessly, and his cock bobbed and smacked on his stomach.

"Hold still," Kenny murmured and then slicked up his fingers again.

"God, Kenny, it's good. I mean... it's making me crazy, but it's *good*!"

"I know, baby. I know."

Kenny had originally planned to use the three different plugs in the bag on himself. With Gif, he would have made a sex show out of it, displayed how wanton and exhibitionistic he was. But with Gif... he hadn't trusted Gif to see to Kenny's pleasure at all, so that was the only way Kenny was going to get off.

But Will would want to be a part of this.

So he greased his fingers up and slipped them behind him, surprised at how tight he was, how resistant.

Oh God, this was going to be awesome!

He closed his eyes, lost in the sweetness of the ache and burn, and then Will cupped his face.

"Good?" Will asked, voice husky, and Kenny nodded, keeping his eyes closed.

"Gonna be better in a second," he said. He arched his back, undulated, fucked his fingers a little more, and realized he was grinding up against Will's thigh. Oh God. He was going to come before he even mounted if he kept this up.

He pulled his fingers out reluctantly and wiped them on the little cloth. Then, as quickly as he could, he straddled Will and spent a moment in that position worshiping the heaving muscles of Will's chest and stomach.

"Still feel good?" he asked, and Will nodded, whining a little and arching his back. "Awesome," Kenny continued. "It's gonna feel good to me too. *So* good. So now you know, don't worry. Don't worry about hurting me, I control the pressure and the speed. Don't worry about being too big—you feel that stretch, that ache and burn?"

Will whimpered.

"*Exactly*," Kenny hissed, positioning Will's cock at his entrance and pushing against it. "Ahhhh… God!"

Will hissed too, thrusting up slowly to help, and for a moment, there was the slow, oh so goddamned slow, burn and glide of that fat, full *thing* thrusting into Kenny, filling him up, making him, gasp, shudder, and—

"*Omigod!*" Kenny screamed. "So good! Don't stop!"

Will grabbed Kenny's hips for purchase and kept thrusting up slowly, steadily, until *holy Christ,* he was seated all the way into the depths of Kenny's body.

Their eyes locked, and Will said, "Good?"

Kenny's hands shook as he tried to smooth them over Will's chest. "Great," he breathed. "Great. Now out!" Slowly, oh so slowly, Kenny lifted himself up, stroking Will's cock with his muscles until the head stretched his rim. Kenny hovered there for a minute before sliding back down again.

"*Omigod*!" they said in tandem, and then Will pulled back and Kenny lifted up and they started the whole cycle over again.

Slow, so slow, wonderfully, excruciatingly slow, until Will grasped Kenny's hips hard and started to beg.

"Faster, Kenny, can we go faster, God, I've really got to start going—"

"Fuck me, dammit! Fucking faster!" Kenny begged, and oh, that did it. Will held him in place and started to piston his hips in short, hard strokes, as fast as he could manage, and Kenny... oh hell, he just kept himself *right there* and Will nailed his gland, stretched him wide, and hit him again and again and again and—

"Grab your cock!" Will ordered. "I want to feel you!"

Kenny could barely do it, he was so high on arousal and pleasure and oh damn, his hand, stroking hard, and Will fucking him, *fucking him* as he'd never been filled before, and....

Kenny started to shake and then Will started to shake and Kenny tilted his head back and howled, "Yes, oh hell yes, *omigod*, Will, fuck me so fucking good!"

And Will just howled, no words. "*Aurugh!*"

Their climaxes—together, beautiful—exploded behind Kenny's eyes, inside his body, rocking them both, clenching them together. Will stayed buried so deeply inside Kenny's ass, Kenny wasn't sure how he'd lived his whole life without Will Lafferty there the whole damned time.

He collapsed on top of Will, their sweaty bodies cooling as they just breathed, coming down from the high. Kenny opened his eyes and realized that Will's eyes, plain, average brown, wide and deep, were peering at him curiously, looking for insights into his soul.

"That was amazing," Will said, no question, and Kenny had to smile. Here, when they were together, skin to skin, Will had a whole lot of confidence Kenny never would have suspected when he'd first seen him, shambling, frustrated, and hypnotized by a shiny thing in the road.

"It has *never* been that good," Kenny told him soberly. He was trying to say something important, but he wasn't sure if he was up to the scary words when there wasn't a phone between them.

Will's grin turned sort of wry. "Man, if I'd known it was going to be this good, I would have started doing it a long time ago!"

Kenny thought about that notion he'd had, when Will had been drunk and vulnerable, of taking him and doing wicked things with that big, solid, awesome body, and giving Will the space to just forget about it. Just forget about *him* because it was just sex, and really, who needed to remember every time you had sex?

His next words to Will were unexpectedly passionate. "I'm *glad* it was now." He rested his cheek on Will's chest and moved a little. Will's body slid out of his, and he missed the connection at the same time the mess of it made him shiver. God, he felt more replete than he ever had in his life.

"Not sooner?" Will asked idly, and Kenny felt Will's fingers ruffling through his hair.

"If it had happened sooner, I wouldn't have known what I had." Kenny's voice broke a little, and he didn't want to go there. He cleared his throat, and the ding from the kitchen told him dinner was ready. He went to roll off and Will tightened his arms around his shoulders.

"It'll keep," Will said mildly. "It's not going to burn just yet. What are you thinking about that got you so sad?"

Kenny looked up at him and smiled, and he couldn't keep the wistfulness out of the smile. "I was going to seduce you that first night," he confessed. "I figured I could be your dirty little secret."

To his surprise, Will laughed. "That's *great*! Really? You had designs on me? That's *awesome*!"

Kenny narrowed his eyes, but he had a hard time compressing his mouth into a line. "You're taking it awfully well."

When Will smiled, his cheeks popped up and deep grooves cut into his cheeks. Between his size and his damned inescapable sincerity, it made him look like some sort of celebratory god.

"But don't you see? You wanted me! You didn't even know me and you wanted me. That's *awesome*—I sort of assumed you just humored me until, you know, I tried to hang from your tonsils by my tongue."

Kenny's chest shook, but he couldn't even laugh. "Will...." And he couldn't say it out loud. He couldn't. It was too precious, too raw, and the thought of accidentally crushing it was just too painful.

Will mauled his head in a massive, sweaty hand, and Kenny received a gentle benediction on his forehead. "I love you, you know that, right?"

"I'm new and shiny," Kenny whispered, which was unfair, perhaps, because Will had never even *seen* the gold lamé shirt, but he knew his biggest fear, and here they were, naked, dripping with each other, and that fear was going to peep out over his shoulder and stick out its tongue. "It's easy to love me."

"Yes," Will said, and Kenny looked up sharply to see a smile that was all kindness. "It's extremely easy to love you, and I'm lazy. Why would I go looking for someone else to love when this perfect person is right here, and he likes me too?"

"Love," Kenny corrected, because he couldn't stand for the words to come out of Will's mouth sounding that weak. "I love you."

Will sealed it with a kiss, and Kenny kissed him back, and they might have had really messy sloppy seconds, except after a few more minutes of kissing, the smoke alarm went off and they *had* to get out of bed.

They ordered pizza that night. Kenny broke out the ice cream, which they ate from the carton while sitting next to each other on the couch, watching *Pitch Black* on the Syfy channel. For once neither of them cracked their laptops, and Kenny didn't even think about pulling out his stylus.

It was sort of a celebration.

SPACES AND HESITATIONS

THE THIRD Saturday in July would have been such a lovely day to have a lie-in. The air conditioner was on, which meant it was going to be hot, but not yet. Kenny snuggled next to his back, and Will's phone was tucked under the pillow with *Shadow Unit 12*, which he'd been reading in his spare time. (He was also reading erotica in his spare and not-so-spare time, because hey, newly discovered penis here. He was pretty sure he'd be fucking Kenny raw if he didn't keep trying for that gold medal in wanking.)

But he didn't *have* to wank, not today, with Kenny here, except his phone kept ringing, and… oh shit.

"Kenny," Will mumbled.

"More?" Kenny asked hopefully.

Will propped himself up on one elbow. They'd fallen asleep after round three the night before, and Kenny looked… well, debauched, really.

Used.

He had a white streak of Will's come running down his chin and another clot matting his hair. The, uhm, "accoutrements," as Will still thought of them, were sitting on the end table, awaiting a thorough washing, probably in the dishwasher, and the towel underneath Will's hips was still a little sticky.

It had been a *very* good night.

And now it was over.

"Kenny, wake up. That's your phone too."

"Aw fuck," Kenny mumbled, running his hand down his face. He reached blindly for the charger, knocking one of the graduated plugs on the ground and startling Princess, who slept like a furry sandbag at their feet. "God. It's Mom."

Which was who happened to be calling Will too.

Will's conversation took longer.

"Hey, Mom—"

"Were you coming over today?"

"Uh, yeah. Sleeping in—"

"I noticed. Honey, you'd better get a move on. It's already ninety out there."

Ugh.

"Okay. Yeah. Lemme shower." Oh crap—Will had biked to Kenny's the night before. "Kenny can drop me off."

There was a weighted silence right then, in which Will heard Kenny say, "Okay, Mom. Talk to you next week. Have a nice trip," before his mom spoke again.

"So, Kenny. When are you going to bring him by?"

Will grimaced. Ugh. Sex and friendship? They'd been doing that for weeks. They'd work together, watch television, and sometime between dinner and the time the lights went out, they ended up in bed, doing all the stuff Will had been watching on porn only better, because hearing Kenny scream out his name (or, usually, just make sounds like "*Gunghhh!*") was something that would *never* grow old.

But this whole "what is the relationship" thing. It seemed that by going from friends to lovers, they'd sort of bypassed all of the subcategories of "lover." Were they lovers? Were they fuck buddies? (*Please, no, please, no, please, no....*) Were they boyfriends? (*Please, yes, please, yes, please, yes, please, yes, please, please, please, please, please....*)

"When he's not busy," Will hedged, glaring at Kenny. Kenny wasn't meeting his eyes, though, and Will suppressed a sigh. "I promise, when it's time—"

"So when he's actually committing to you," his mother said shortly—right when Kenny pulled the covers down and started licking around Will's naked cock with delicate little laps.

"Later, Mom," Will breathed, trying very hard to keep his voice normal. "I'll be there in an hour!" and with that, he hit End Call.

Kenny chuckled evilly and engulfed his hard-on in one gulp, and Will's eyes rolled to the back of his head and his conversation with his mother was forgotten.

BUT HE remembered it as he was hauling on his clothes after the world's quickest shower, waiting for Kenny to do the same.

"What kind of work are you supposed to be doing?" he asked, grabbing a clean pair of socks out of Kenny's drawer while eyeballing the room for his other tennis shoe.

"What?" Kenny still looked a little out of it as he came out of the shower, rubbing fitfully at his hair.

"I told my mom you were working today and that's why you couldn't visit. I'm a horrible liar—give me a lie!"

Kenny grunted. "Is it really that important?" he asked, his gaze wandering around the room. "It's under the bed, Will."

"Oh. That's better than the top of the dresser," Will said philosophically. Which was where it had been the day before. "And yes, it's important. *I love you.* And I'm a big whiny mama's boy, and you need to meet my mommy!"

Of all things, *that* seemed to snap Kenny out of his postsexual fugue. (Will had nailed him until he lost the powers of speech—and yes, Will was damned proud of that.)

"You know… I'm not that great at parents—"

"Really?" Will did his best to look stern. "When was the last time you met any?" He knew the answer to this, oh yes he did.

"Six months before never?" And that the lilt at the end of his voice was a sad and obvious attempt to take out the sting.

Shocker! "Okay, you do realize my mom met Denise, don't you?"

Kenny's mouth dropped open. "Whatserface? The one who wanted to go wine tasting and didn't believe you when you said you were gay?"

"That's the one. And we went out to the movies one Saturday, and I made her meet my mother."

Something must have been socially backward about that statement, because Kenny was getting a crafty look like Will had won this argument for him.

"*See!*" he crowed. "I *told* you that you gave her reason to—"

"I bring *all* of my friends to meet my mother!" Will growled. "Because until now, she's been my best friend. And I know that's stupid and I *know* it's backwards, but—"

"It's not," Kenny protested. Will thought it was probably Kenny's long habit of defending Will even from himself that made him do that. "In fact, I think it's sweet!"

"Well, I notice you don't want me to meet *your* parents," Will snapped, because the part of Kenny's conversation that he'd actually *heard* had stung.

"That's different," Kenny told him with a little sniff.

"Yeah?"

"I don't like my parents as much as you like your mother." He said it with a curled lip and a sort of superiority that made Will roll his eyes.

"News to me. Why not?" Kenny's dresser sat under the window, and Will had at *least* remembered to put his wallet there. He retrieved it now, warm from the sunshine, and slid it into his back pocket.

Kenny had fished out his own clothes while they'd been talking, and now he slid his technicolor boxers up his moderately hairy legs and adjusted himself in them. Just watching him do that made Will horny again.

"They're... I mean, they don't make conversation," Kenny said as though trying to find words. "I mean, I was sort of a failure, you know? Everyone else in their family either went into the military or did the full-court-press college, and I went to vocational school. I think they're embarrassed."

"Have they ever *said* they're embarrassed?" Because *then* Will would have to get mad at somebody. He could do it too!

"No," Kenny responded, smiling slightly. "Well, my douchey brother did, but my folks didn't. I just... you know, folks retired, like to roam the country. No time for offspring who aren't spawning. Besides, your mom gets your whole comic-book thing—"

Will snorted. "I never said that. I mean, it would be *nice* if she got it, but she doesn't *really* get it. But she likes *me*, so she tries. Just like I don't get what her relationship with my father was like or why she won't date again, but I like *her*, so I try. It's not a perfect relationship, Kenny, but it's my *mom*. And...." He realized they'd squared off, and he hated the idea of fighting. He stood up behind Kenny and nuzzled his ear. "You're becoming more important than she is, you know?"

Kenny grunted. "Yeah?" And he sounded interested in that, as though it mattered to him.

"Yeah! So it would be nice if you'd set her mind to rest about her baby boy before you sort of took over as front and center in his life. I mean, isn't that what marriage ceremonies are all about?"

Kenny jerked in his arms. "We're not getting married!" he protested.

Will sighed.

"Not when you won't meet my mother!"

Kenny sighed too. "I can't today," he said. "No! Really! Princess has a V-E-T appointment"—he looked around furtively, and Princess twitched her fluffy white tail and drooled on the bed in her sleep—"complete with a meet with the groomers, and if we don't get some of that fur off before the end of the summer, she's going to get heatstroke and die."

Oh—well, that, at least, was legitimate. "She wouldn't if she'd stop sleeping in the sun," Will muttered. It was sort of scary, actually. She'd lie in a convenient sunspot with her little pugged mouth open, panting. Kenny brushed her all the time, and every time he did, he'd have enough fur for what looked to be another damned cat. A groomer was a good idea—Will just didn't know it had been coming. "And you should have told me last night. I would have brought the car. I'll have to ride to my mom's as it is."

Oh hell.

"In this heat?" Kenny protested, turning around in his arms, but Will shrugged.

"I didn't say I wasn't going to steal a crapload of waters," he admitted.

Kenny pursed his lips. "I'm sorry. I should have told you before you came over—you're right. I just...." Kenny smiled shyly then, and all of the remembered tension was forgotten. "You know. Just got happy you were coming over."

"Well, I'm glad you didn't have to work late last night," Will said, and he meant it. The night before, Kenny had texted him and told him to stay home because it would be a late night. He didn't have many, but Will respected that he had to have *some*, or he wouldn't be able to keep going in his job. He'd confessed to Will that the more productive he was, the better assignments he got—and he didn't like the stuff on the bottom rung of the ladder.

"It's worth it," Kenny told him, smiling softly into his eyes.

Will lowered his mouth for a kiss, and Kenny responded tenderly. When Will pulled back, he said, "I love you," and Kenny pecked him on the cheek.

"Mmto," he mumbled.

Will grunted unhappily. "I'm about to ride my frickin' bike in the soul-melting heat and that's what you got for me?"

Kenny looked down between them like he could study Will's thick middle for some sort of answer. "I love you," he said, like a schoolkid with his toe in the dirt, apologizing to the girl he'd just shoved in the mud.

But he did say it, and Will knew he wouldn't have said it if he didn't mean it.

"Close enough," he conceded grimly. "Now give me another kiss and send me out naked into the inferno."

KENNY HAD three big bottles of water in his freezer, and he shoved them *all* in Will's backpack so Will could make the eight-mile journey without just keeling the hell over. Will got to his mother's house hot and sweaty and irritable, and by the time he mowed her lawn, he was in no mood to discuss his boyfriend troubles.

"The vet's?" Anne didn't do sarcasm just like Will didn't do sarcasm. "Really? Will, that seems awfully thin—"

Will held up his wrist, where Princess had laid into him as he was hefting her large fluffy body into the cat carrier.

"Oh," his mom finished. "Okay. Yeah, the vet's office was a real thing. I get it. But really, how long have you two been together?"

"About a month," Will said. "I'm pretty sure Kenny's surprised it's lasted this long."

He was sitting in her air-conditioned living room while the fan blasted his cooling BO all over his mom's house, and he didn't care. God, it was hot outside. Maybe he could get Kenny to meet him at the gym later—they went to the same one—just so they could swim in the pool.

"Why's he so gun-shy?" she asked musingly. She didn't sound judgy, because, hey, Will's *mom*, who had pretty much accepted "Mom, I'm gay" with a giggle and a prayer, and she didn't judge.

Mostly she just sounded curious, but then, so was Will.

"Well, when I met him, he'd just had an ugly breakup with his boyfriend," Will hedged, because that was about as far as he wanted to go into their meeting right now. "And I get the feeling…." It was hard to put into words, the feeling Will kept getting. The way Kenny kept looking at him incredulously when he said, "I love you!" or falling all over him when he did the dishes or helped with dinner. He was grateful, but it was more than that. It was like all of the small things that were important to Kenny—the place settings, the happy feline, the pretty house—were things Kenny had always assumed he would have to have on his *own*. Every time Will showed an interest in them, they became somehow special. Like they were another item added to the list of reasons Will might not leave.

"I get the feeling he's been discarded a lot," Will said thoughtfully. "I mean, not in horrible ways—or, well, until his last boyfriend came back to try to steal his bike—but, you know. Like the things that were important to him have never been important to the guys he's been with."

His mom made a sudden little sound, one of complete understanding, and Will looked at her in surprise.

"Oh," she said simply. "Okay, I get it. Well, you bring him by when you can get him to come, honey." And then, just like that, she dropped the subject and they spent the rest of the time gossiping about how Aunt Cara's assistant had brought Cara a big vat of fresh-squeezed lemonade when she found out Cara loved the stuff, and if that wasn't a labor of love, Anne didn't know what was.

"But what will Cara do if Nina's really in love with her?" Will asked, suddenly fearful for this Nina person whom he'd never met. What if Cara rebuffed her? What if Cara really wasn't (as Will's mom suspected) ready to play for her home team? How awful would that be, to pine and pine for someone you were *sure* you'd be perfect with, only to find that it was never meant to be?

The thought made Will's stomach a little squirmy and his chest ache a little too much, so when he got Kenny's text that said, *Have mom drop you off at the gym. Let's go swimming!* he was more than ready to accept it as a sign of kismet.

Kenny had read his mind from across town. Will was going to have to put his restless thoughts to bed and hope for the best.

WILL'S MOM was happy to throw his bike in the back of the car and drop him at the gym, and the swim was *great*. They stayed in the water, just talking, until the shadows grew long and the mosquitoes threatened to devour them whole as an appetizer, and then they put the bike on the rack of the tiny smart car and went back to Kenny's house, where they spent all their weekends.

They had salads for dinner and then spent a long, glorious, *productive* evening meshing their imaginations on their project. While Will was waiting for Kenny to draw, he caught up on his web clients, and Kenny looked over his shoulder approvingly.

"Business is growing," he said, sounding smug, and Will nodded.

"It's getting there." But not fast enough. He didn't want to tell Kenny that, because he spent most of his nights at Kenny's house. God, hadn't Gif been a freeloader enough? That was the *last* thing he wanted Kenny to think.

"So, ready to get off the teaching train yet?" Kenny asked hopefully.

Will gave an inelegant little snort. "Hardly. In fact"—and he checked his e-mail—"I've got a few interviews lined up in the last week of July."

"Now? Don't schools around here start two weeks into August?"

Will looked from his computer to where Kenny sat, his adorable little hooked nose wrinkled in disbelief. Will nodded and reached out and touched his finger to the end of it, just because he could.

"Well, *yeah*," he said, grinning. "I'm *lucky*, because usually they don't interview until a week before. God forbid we hire anyone before, like, the first day of school, right?"

"Ugh, that's vile. They don't do that in my mom's school district."

Yeah. Davis. Davis had a lot more money than any of the school districts Will had applied to. "Well, in Davis they have a more solid tax base," Will told him, although he was pretty sure it was something Kenny already knew.

Kenny yawned and stretched. "I don't want to talk about school right now," he said plaintively. "It's been too good a night and we've gotten too much done. Do you want to start working on the website tomorrow?"

Wow. This was really happening. They were really going to do this!

"Absolutely! But maybe first, we finish one more chapter."

They got to bed late—past one in the morning, and Will, for one, was damned tired. In the dark, Kenny snuggled up to him and they kissed warmly, but Will's eyes fell closed, and Kenny tucked against his shoulder, and they fell asleep soon after that.

THEY SPENT the whole next day together, just like they had the month prior, but this time, Will listened.

He said "I love you" three times that day.

Kenny didn't say it once.

It wasn't a reason to pout or to end the relationship or even to argue.

But it did leave Will wondering when the other shoe was going to drop off the dresser to under the bed, and if he'd notice when it did.

THE SONG changed. "I Promise You I Will" by Depeche Mode came on, and a breeze flirted over the tops of the wedding crowd.

"Mm," Kenny sighed, and Will settled into the dance some more.

"You like the song?"

"I promise you, I promise you…." Kenny sang, and Will thought that yes, one way or another, Kenny had made promises and kept them.

BECAUSE SAD

"MOMMM," KENNY complained, but he really wasn't arguing *that* hard.

"Kenny, your brother is coming home in two weeks. It would be great if you could visit."

"Great for whom?" Kenny asked drily, and his mother blew out a breath.

"Well, great for me, for one," she said, the science-teacher steel in her voice unbending enough for Kenny to hear that yes, she did realize that Joey could be a complete prick, and no, there wasn't much she could do about it.

Kenny had come out of the closet when he was twelve years old, fully expecting his very liberal parents to be completely on his side.

And they had been.

His older brother, Joey, who'd already been in the ROTC and primed to join the army as soon as he left high school?

Joey had a fit.

Of course, it had been in the height of Don't Ask/Don't Tell, and suddenly Joey had this… this… *undesirable* right there in his own family. Their parents had been all PFLAG and gay rights and "Taste the Rainbow," and Joey had been, "If someone tries to bash you, don't expect me to fucking help."

Of course it was *Davis*, which was like a liberal oasis in the Republican desert that was Sacramento, so Kenny could have been revered as an iconic god. He'd sort of shrugged *that* burden aside, of course, because seriously, who the hell wanted *that* to hang around his neck through high school? But he *had* been allowed to sort of snark in peace, and that was all he'd really desired out of his formative years.

And if he missed the days when he and Joey used to build blanket forts and make big project cards for their mother for Mother's Day, well, Hawaii was a long way away, and Kenny never had to visit and be reminded that Joey wasn't ever going to do that with him again. Small price to pay, really, for his sweet little house in the shitty suburb and the sweet guy who came to visit five nights out of seven.

Although Kenny was really starting to miss him on the two nights he wasn't there.

"So, are you coming to visit?" his mom asked, and Kenny let out a sigh.

"Yeah."

"Are you bringing Gif?"

Oh shit.

"Gif and I broke up at the beginning of May," he told her, checking under the foil to see if their dinner was getting close to done, and cringing. In spite of the early August heat, he was making pot roast with all the fixings. Yeah, he was cranking the AC especially high today, but dammit, sometimes a guy just got tired of salad.

Besides, for all that Will was nice about the salads, Kenny had seen the fast-food containers in the bottom of his backpack, and he was pretty sure Will stopped at McDonald's for a chicken sandwich on the way home, which meant that sometimes the big guy needed something a little more substantial to keep his strength up. Kenny had no problems cooking for his man if that was what it took to help him keep his strength (among other things) emphatically up.

"Kenny! That's three months ago! You couldn't have told us then?"

Oh God. After watching Will's sweet—and yet weirdly autonomous—devotion to his mother, he felt like a first-class heel. It wasn't his *mother's* fault Joey was a prime prick who had tried to make Kenny feel like his gayness—and his choice of profession—made him a prize-winning loser. Besides, that was probably just something brothers did to you, right?

"Well, he wasn't that important to me in the first place," Kenny said, holding Will close to his mental vest for some reason. "I'll let you know when I find someone who won't leave when the shiny is gone."

"Kenny—"

"Gotta go, Mom, the roast is burning—"

"That's a blatant fabrication and you know it!"

"Bye!"

Kenny hit End Call, leaned against the counter, and sighed. God, his mom deserved a better son. In fact, she deserved someone like Will.

Hell. *Kenny* deserved someone like Will. Wouldn't it be great if Kenny could trust, for once and for all, that they'd both have him for a while?

WILL SHOWED up a little late, and Kenny had plenty of time to talk himself into the whole "Will, do you want to meet my perfectly nice parents and my douche-bag big brother?" thing before he heard the car in the driveway. Kenny was wondering why he hadn't ridden his bike when he saw the man of his dreams slogging from the big brown-purple land yacht to the porch, wearing an off-season corduroy suit with a hideous avocado tie.

He was smiling tentatively, and he had a bottle of white wine, which Kenny particularly liked, and he came through the door so bursting with beginning-of-August heat that Kenny started sweating the minute his foot hit the floor.

"You're late, and oh my *God*!" He took the bottle of wine and set it in the fridge, nagging all the way. "Go change! Go shower! It's 108 out there—go do something besides hang out in my house in that suit and drive up the temperature!"

Will laughed, and Kenny followed him down the hall to dig out the sleep shorts and T-shirt Will had left that week. They'd just been washed, and Kenny had started a drawer for him so Will could leave a toothbrush and anything else he might want right there within fingertips' reach.

"Go jump in the shower," Kenny admonished as Will shed the sport coat with the faded leather patches at the elbows. "My God, where were you? Was it like a...." Oh God. Will had said he might have a few this summer. "Was it a job interview?" he asked, praying it hadn't been.

Will beamed at him. "Yeah! I got the job too, which was fortunate, because I was about to have to move in with my mother."

"You got the job?" Kenny almost wailed, and Will shucked his boxers as quickly as he could, seeing as they got stuck on the sweat around his thighs.

"Well, yeah—you don't sound happy?"

"You... I mean, you're almost done with the website. Are you going to have time to do that?" *Way to go, Kenny. Way to sound like a self-involved douche when that's not the real reason you don't want him to have that job, and you know it!*

Will grimaced. "Man, it's gonna have to go on the back burner— I'm sorry. But I've got all those other clients—I mean, it's going to be almost like two full-time jobs for a while. I'm so—"

"Don't be sorry," Kenny snapped, setting that horrible, sweaty, bulky, disgusting, gross shackle of a corduroy suit on the hanger. "Just don't take the job. You've worked so hard these last three months building clients, getting our own site started. Why can't you just do that?"

Will sighed and walked into the bathroom and turned on the shower. The stupid Neanderthal didn't even wait for the hot water to come out, he just stepped into it cold, whooped like a mountain man, used Kenny's soap quickly in all his private places and on his hair, and jumped out as soon as the rinsing was done. Kenny hung the suit up on the side of the bedroom door so it could air out, and then waited for him like a goober because... because this entire idea *hurt* him.

When Will came out, he was wrapped in a towel, just like the time—the first time—they'd done the thing, the big thing, with the other thing. It was weird. Kenny couldn't think "sex toy" anymore, because as much fun as he and Will had in bed, none of it seemed to be playing around.

Kenny looked at him now and realized that this wasn't playing around either. This wasn't Gif signing up for extra shifts because he needed the money and the elderly people in the home he worked for didn't care if he was crankier than they were. This was Will, and he took this job seriously, and Kenny needed to be honest.

He'd learned so much about Will in the past three months. It was time to show he'd done his homework.

He walked into Will's space, liking the cool feel that came off his skin after the shower, and placed a gentle kiss on a pale shoulder. He thought if Will was a sun worshipper, he'd probably have freckles, but he wasn't. Classic farmer's tan. Kenny liked the paleness—it was secret skin, just for Kenny, the same way Will's powerhouse sexuality was just for Kenny too. Only Kenny had been bent over the bed and pounded into the mattress, and only Kenny had tasted Will's semen, bursting into his mouth while sunshine poured over Will's naked body like a blessing.

And only Kenny knew how tender, how open Will's heart really was, and why this was a really bad idea.

"Will? Baby? Maybe, for you, the teaching thing is sort of no bueno."

Will laughed. "Kenny? Baby? I have the teaching certificate and everything. I mean, I'm *good* at it. I love grade-schoolers!" Will's lopsided smile was goofy and true. "You know, the stupid jokes, the excitement about everything. It's my peer group!"

Kenny laughed because that was the Gospel of Will right there—he really was an overgrown fifth grader, in the best sense of the word. And that was going to kill him.

Kenny tried really hard not to feel like shit, because besides being Will's first sex, he was going to have to be Will's first broken heart—in this, at least. "Will, you know how you liked Harry Potter and you shared?"

Will nodded and put his hands on Kenny's waist, probably because he just liked to touch. "Well, yeah. But this is public school. They don't care if the kids are reading porn as long as they're reading, you know!" He paused and giggled. "Not that I'd, you know, teach porn."

Kenny grimaced. "They don't care if the kids are reading *het* porn, sweetheart. And that's the problem."

Will blinked at him owlishly. "What? I mean, the porn thing was only a joke—"

"Yeah, but the gay thing isn't. And you're gay. And all you have to do, just once, is mention your boyfriend, and it doesn't even have to be to a kid. It could be to another teacher, and a kid hears. And if you talk about 'your friend Kenny' too much, people are going to suspect, and if anyone asks you, what are you going to say?"

Will's face grew hurt and shuttered. "I'll say it's none of their business," he said, but he sounded angry and defensive, even to Kenny.

"Yeah. And then they'll know. And it might not be a big deal, because things are getting better. But this whole area is pretty freaking conservative, so it might. It might be a big deal, and you know what teaching is like before tenure...." Kenny's mom was a teacher. Thirty years of tenure, head of the science department—but Kenny had grown up hearing about it and knowing.

"They can let you go for anything," Will said, his voice dropping sadly, like he knew this already and had just put two and two together.

"Will, you wear your heart on your sleeve. And I love that about you." *Okay, Kenny, be real.* "I *love* you, and that's one of the things I love most." Kenny swallowed. "But you're not the most socially aware person on the planet."

Will smiled gamely. "But... but public school. It should be fine as long as I—"

"Switch your pronouns and pretend you're not in love with a man and sound out the staff room carefully to see if you've got any ultraconservatives in there who think the GSA is an excuse for kids to have sex."

"I mean, maybe if I just keep to myself—"

"And don't share any part of you, because you're afraid?"

"But—"

Kenny closed his eyes and framed Will's dear, open face with both hands. "Honey, even *I* know you don't teach evolution in a fundamentalist church school."

Will's eyes were bright and red-rimmed, and he swallowed. "But Kenny, I've got to pay rent. I mean, it's what I went to school to *do!*"

"But you've got the whole web design thing—"

"But it's not big enough. Moving into my mother's house, Kenny—seriously. I was going to have to borrow money from her to make it to my next rent."

Kenny swallowed and turned away. "Well, move in here."

"No."

Kenny turned around, outraged. "*No*? You're here almost every night as it is!"

"And I like that. But I'm not moving in with you because I can't make rent. You'll assume I'm a freeloader, and then, if we even start to make a life together, you'll tell yourself that I just moved in because I needed a place to stay, and you'll lump me in with the asshole who tried to steal your bike."

Kenny fell back, opening his mouth and closing it. He didn't know what to say—it was true. "I... look, I know you're not Gif."

Will sighed and his head drooped a little onto shoulders that were suddenly hunched, like they had been the first night Kenny had taken him out to get drunk.

"I know you do. But you use 'I love you' like your Sunday clothes. You bring them both out for special occasions. I'm pretty sure that's because you never knew if they'd get crapped on or not, but sometimes... sometimes it just hurts, knowing how hard you're trying not to love me as much as I love you."

Once, in a moment of carelessness, Gif closed Princess's big fluffy tail in the bathroom door. He'd felt bad—he wasn't a *monster*—but the sound Princess made when he'd had to open the door had nothing on what came out of Kenny's throat at that moment.

And again, he couldn't argue. He *was* trying not to love Will too much. He *was* saving the words for special occasions. He *did* expect, any day now, for Will to prove as inconstant, as flaky, as untrue, as any other lover he'd ever had.

When so far Will had been anything but.

Kenny turned around to say he was sorry, to say "I love you," to say *anything* so Will wouldn't look so hurt. Will beat him to it.

"Kenny, could you, uhm... see, I'm gonna change and probably just go home. We can celebrate this some other day, okay?"

"No!"

But Will's eyes were bright and his face had flushed crimson, and he looked embarrassed and humiliated, and Kenny didn't have a single thing to say to him to make it better.

"Look, I just, I mean, I know my apartment is crappy and everything, but you know, I'm twenty-eight. I'd like to sort of be able to say I don't live with my mom for as long as possible."

"I think you're too good for the job," Kenny said baldly. "Is that so bad? That I think you're too good to have to go through all that when something you're good at is *right here*, without all the pain?"

Will's smile had a twist on the ends. "That's kind," he said, and Kenny tried not to scream.

"I'm not a kind person. I'm a shitty person. If I was a better person, I wouldn't have brought a sewer rat like Gif home and tried to domesticate him like a house cat. If I was a better person, I wouldn't be hurting you right now—"

"You're a *great* person!" Will defended staunchly, and Kenny turned his back so Will couldn't see him wipe his eyes.

"Then don't go. Stay for dinner. Stay and work. Stay and be my friend. Don't... don't break up with me."

After a breathless quiet, he felt Will at his back, holding his shoulder. Kenny breathed through a pause and then felt a gentle kiss at his temple.

"I'm not breaking up with you. But ask yourself, if I *did*, what would you call me? Would I be your steady lay? Your friend with benefits? You've never put a name to it. I told my mom and aunt Cara I have a boyfriend."

"Your *aunt Cara?*"

Will's arms encircled him from behind, and Kenny leaned his head against his shoulder.

"Yeah, my aunt Cara. She's wanted to meet you for *two months*, just like Mom, and I'm never sure what you're going to do if I ask. Princess can only have so many vet appointments! So think about it. I told my mom I have a boyfriend. What have you told *your* parents?"

Kenny made an uncomfortable sound. "I told them that Gif moved out," he mumbled. "But in my defense, they weren't aware that

Gif had moved *in*." Gif had never wanted to come visit on his once-a-month meetings for lunch.

The big body behind him shook heavily, and then a gentle puff of air in his ear was all he got of Will's laugh.

"They've got to know who I am, Kenny. I'm not going away—unless you keep treating me like I am."

Kenny nodded. "But you're still going? Tonight, I mean?"

Will sighed weightily enough to riffle Kenny's hair. "I hurt a little. I need some man time to recover, right?"

God. "You're the only man I've ever met who's strong enough to admit that," Kenny told him, trying not to let his voice break. "I'll go put some dinner in a thing for you."

He broke away then and made his way into the kitchen. He cut off a big chunk of roast and ladled some vegetables into a plastic container and then put it in a little lunch box. By the time he was done, Will had come out from the bedroom wearing the basketball shorts and T-shirt Kenny had just washed for him. He kept a pair of flip-flops there too, and he had his keys in his hand.

"Hey, you don't have to—" Will started, and Kenny tried a smile.

"No, hon. At least let me feed you, okay?"

"But you're really going to trust me with the lunch box?" Will asked, and his smile looked a little better than Kenny's felt.

"I have to," Kenny said, proud of the fact that his voice didn't wobble. "This way I'm sure you'll be back." And that was it for dignity. He thrust the box into Will's hands and turned his back to put away the dinner he knew he wouldn't eat. By the time he looked up, he'd already heard the door close—not slam, mind you, because Will was a grown-up, but close—and Princess was bitching at him plaintively.

"Meow, meow, meow," Kenny muttered. "Yeah, yeah, yeah. I just let him go. I'm a schmuck. But he's the he-man, right? He's the one who beat up the bad guy and did the kiss. Shouldn't he want to fight for me a little?"

Princess got up on her back legs and deliberately extended her claws into Kenny's knee. Then she pulled.

"Ow, you *bitch*!" Kenny snapped. He bent down to disentangle his flesh from her weapons, and she retracted her claws. She swiped his hand hard enough to leave a blood trail, then ran off, hissing.

Oh. My. God. It was bad enough he'd taken the lunchbox. Apparently he'd taken the cat's affection too.

And Kenny's heart. Let's not forget that, right?

Kenny couldn't work on the project that night—even if he and Will worked independently, just opening his computer to the pages he needed to finish made him all hiccuppy and stupid. He thought about going to the gym to do laps, but he'd already worked out during his lunch hour, and, well, it was 108 degrees outside and not getting any cooler. He sat and watched television mindlessly until he realized he was watching the Syfy channel and that Will wasn't there to watch it with him, and he didn't even know if Will had a TV in his self-proclaimed crappy little apartment.

And then Kenny realized he didn't even know where Will's crappy little apartment *was*. He knew it was within biking distance, but beyond that, he had a vague impression of somewhere around San Juan and Fair Oaks, so about three or four miles away.

He sat up suddenly.

God, that was a shitty ride. It hadn't even occurred to him what a shitty ride that was, and all of the potential for disaster, and getting hit by a car, and all that scary stuff, and Will never wore a helmet.

His heart roared in his ears and his breath caught short and he was having a retroactive panic attack for all of the stupid things Will had done when Kenny wasn't there to watch out for him. He *had* to talk to him right now.

Will, I want you to buy a bicycle helmet.

What in the hell?

Look, baby, just promise me, okay? I'll buy you one.

My head's too big. None of them fit.

I'll go to a specialty shop.

It's like 24" around.

I DON'T GIVE A FUCK I'M BUYING YOU A HELMET!

Oooooooookaaaay?????

Please. Just, when you come over tomorrow, drive the car.

All right. Is this a sneaky way to get me to commit to coming over tomorrow?

You were coming over anyway, weren't you?

Yes, of course. We're not breaking up, Kenny. I still love you.

THEN WHY AREN'T YOU HERE?

Because sad.

Next time you're sad, stay here. Next time you're happy, stay here. STAY HERE.

You're awfully brave from behind a phone.

*sob * I know. Why can't I be brave in real life?

You are. You can be. I'm going to bed now. I love you, good night.

Kenny didn't argue about it only being nine thirty. He was going to bed too.

I love you too. Good night.

He sat for another half hour and watched TV. When he realized it had been paused the whole time, he got disgusted with himself, grabbed the newest Jim Butcher, and crawled into bed.

As he was getting comfortable, he saw Will's suit—his hopeless, stupid, sweaty corduroy suit—and he whimpered.

He was right about the job. He knew that.

But Will was right about the "I love you." Why would Will want to listen to life advice from a guy who wasn't invested? And as for Will fighting harder, well, Will had fought plenty hard. Kenny was a perfectly capable man. He could mow his own lawn (although Will was good at it) and chop his own wood (although that was really ecologically unsound, so he didn't do it), and he probably could have beaten Gif in a fistfight because Gif was a big whiner and would have gone down the first time Kenny's fist connected with his nose. But Kenny didn't have to do any of that, because Will did it for him. In fact, Will *wanted* to do it for him, and maybe, just maybe, along with making dinner and ordering the drapes, Kenny could possibly say some "I love yous" and some "I don't care about your income, I want your company and your forever and please move in with mes."

And Kenny could definitely meet the guy's mother.

It was a thought.

One that plagued him as he lay in bed and tried really hard to sleep.

His eyes were drying out.

With a sigh, he got up and grabbed the suit off the door and came back to bed, laying it in Will's spot, legs out like a pretend man. He took the hangar out and set it on the end table, then laid his head on the still-damp shoulder.

He could smell Will's sweat as he fell asleep.

"YOU LOOK like hell," Cam said, eyeballing him sourly. Of course, Cam was still designing how-to pamphlets for new hires, which could make anyone sour. He was good at it, Kenny had realized lately. He'd probably be good at lots of things, but his personal life was what made him happy, even when it didn't.

Kenny was storyboarding a segment for the company's next training video. For sheer glamor, Kenny's assignment won, and Kenny wondered if Cam sort of resented the hell out of him for that, but other than that, he'd been a pretty decent cubicle mate.

"Yeah," Kenny mumbled. "Boyfriend troubles."

"You're gay? Hm."

Kenny looked over his shoulder to see Cam wrinkling his nose like he hadn't known this little tidbit before. After this many months of watching Cam's jowly face take on every expression from a scowl to a sort of glowy homeboy smile, Kenny could never figure out how he got *one* ex-wife, much less almost three, but that wasn't really Kenny's business, was it?

"You didn't judge me by my clothes?" Kenny asked, almost idly. It didn't look like Cam was going to freak out about it, so maybe he could joke a little.

Cam shrugged. "No, not really. Kids these days—you all dress bright."

Oh—so he *had* noticed his cubicle mate a little. All those Dr Peppers must have paid off. "My speech? I never gave it away once?"

Cam's rolled eyes were almost an abomination in that sincere face. "Man, I try not to judge. And it's not like we've really connected. I mean, you can have all the casual conversations you want with a guy, but if he's not going to open up about himself, you're not going to find out. I always got the impression you had loftier goals than this job anyway."

Kenny cocked his head. Wow. Put that way, he sounded like a real asshole. "You mean those Dr Peppers weren't a declaration of undying love?" he asked, smiling, trying to make a better impression, and he got a gruff smile in return.

"Those are definitely appreciated. I just mean, I don't know. You started out trying to set the world on fire, and you did, and now I'm not sure what's left for you to do here. So I figured, you know—you're moving onwards and upwards."

Kenny gaped a little, stunned. Damn. He'd been so busy planning for stability, he'd almost worked and worried his way out of it. "I've got outside projects," he said slowly, "but honestly, I sort of like it here."

"You don't sign up for any of the social stuff," Cam pointed out, and Kenny gasped.

"Well, you know. Gay. In Sacramento."

"Well, yeah, but you could have sounded us out. I mean, you work out during all your lunches, and you're never around for a beer after work. You know. Passing through. I didn't even know you *had* a boyfriend. How long have you been together?"

Kenny thought about it. "It's sort of a weird story," he said, thinking about it. He looked at his watch. "Want to hear it over lunch?"

Cam was decent company—Kenny had already known that. He cleaned up his cubicle, he told the occasional funny joke, and he took time off in the afternoons to coach his kids' soccer league. Kenny had never minded that he got in earlier in order to do this, but now, sitting down and drinking his third vitaminwater with the guy, he had a realization. He'd been so busy trying to prove himself in his job that he'd forgotten that jobs were social places too.

And he'd been so busy trying to prove that he could be friends with Will that he'd forgotten anything he knew about being a good lover.

And he hadn't known that much in the first place.

By the end of lunch, Cam was looking at him with pity. "See, I could have told you that thing with the job was a bad move right there," he said, nodding. "That was my second wife. I tried to tell her that ceramics wouldn't work as a business, but you know what? I hadn't been paying attention to what she'd been doing at work at *all*. Turns out she'd made all these contacts, and she had a business plan that would have put a *Fortune* 500 company to shame. And even if she hadn't? Even if she hadn't done jack shit? Fact was, I *didn't know*—I hadn't made the time investment, you know? I mean, I don't get a say if I'm not really in her life."

"Oh *fuck*," Kenny muttered, because this was pretty much the conclusion he'd come to the night before.

"What? You've got flowers to bring?"

"No," Kenny said miserably, banging his head against the table just hard enough to hurt. "I've got cardboard boxes."

Cam looked suitably puzzled. "Okay, my uncle is gay, and he never said anything about that as a romantic gesture."

And of all things, that made Kenny laugh. "It's not the gay, it's the person," he said kindly. "And would anyone mind if I took the afternoon off?"

"Are you kidding? It's Friday—half the building is going on their August vacation next week. You could take a long weekend and nobody would give a crap if you came back."

Kenny raised his eyebrows and thought of visiting relatives and maybe some extra time in bed. With Will. Naked.

"That's awesome," he said. "I'm going to drop you off and see you Tuesday."

"Yeah? Do I get to know what you're going to do this weekend?"

"Well, for starters I'm going to invite Will to meet my parents and come to the company picnic—when is that, anyway?"

"Labor Day," Cam said drily. "So in a month," he added as they stood up and left money for the tip.

"Fan*tas*tic."

Cam laughed. "Yeah, well, don't be a stranger. You're funny when you're riled."

Kenny wondered if Will felt the same way.

HE SHOWED up at Will's place an hour later, after a stop in shipping and receiving, where they were glad to assign a really gigantic college kid named Artie to help him break down some boxes.

After that, he had to actually *find* the apartment complex, and he was relieved to know that it was shabby but not horrific, because that one place, the one closer to the dentist's office, was a *dump*, and this place was only a block away.

It wasn't bad—brown wood paneled, a basic two-story building. He asked the super for Will's apartment number. It was on the ground floor, which was nice, because Kenny's arms were full of cardboard, and that shit sucked to juggle.

He set all the flattened boxes down against Will's wall, took a deep breath, and knocked.

He could hear Will's heavy tread, and he marked the passage through what looked to be a remarkably small cracker box kind of place until, about two seconds after Kenny knocked, the door opened.

A burst of cool air greeted him, and he had to hold himself back from just rushing the doorway, because sweat was pouring down his back like his neck was a spigot. It was another ungodly hot day.

"Kenny?"

Kenny tried not to glower. God, he sucked at this.

"My name is Kenneth Andrew Scalia. I have a brother named Joseph Kevin, but he's in the service in Hawaii, and he's got a wife and two kids. My parents are Phil and Barbara. Dad owns a small travel agency and Mom taught science until she retired early, last year. They're *constantly* out of town, but the next time they're *not* out of town on a weekend, I'll take you to visit. They don't give a crap about the gay and think I'm too young to have children, so they'll love you."

Kenny took a breath and Will opened his mouth to say something, but Kenny stopped him with an outstretched hand.

"Gif was not my first jerk of a boyfriend. You guessed that, but it was a lot easier to talk about comic books and graphic novels and shows and what happened to us during the day, so I forgot to tell you that I was, like, the guy to cheat on during college. See, I kept going for pretty and hoping for forever. And the problem was, these guys, they were going for pretty and hoping for pretty around the corner. Nothing in my brain was wired to accept a Will Lafferty into my life. But I want you in my life. I want you in my house. I brought boxes. We can start packing the boxes. I'll start moving you *today*. I'll meet your mom anytime. I want her to know I love you too. I want the world to know I love you. I'm just not great at—"

Will reached out, grabbed his collar, and hauled him inside to the blessed, blessed air-conditioning, and Kenny didn't even get a chance to look around before Will's mouth was on his.

The door slammed behind them and Will framed Kenny's face in both hands, pushing him against it. For a moment he was a deep, thick, comforting blanket of kiss.

In this alien and admittedly crappy apartment, Kenny was suddenly home.

He kissed back again and again, climbing Will like a tree. He wrapped his legs around Will's hips and ground up against him, their groins mashing and their chests pressed together tight enough to breathe in tandem.

Kenny leaned back against the door and trusted that Will would hold him as he reached between them with one hand. He got Will's belt undone and then his own, and Will pulled back long enough to gasp, "Bed!"

Kenny whimpered, because the bed seemed too far to walk without touching, but Will grasped him tighter under the thighs, and Kenny held on for dear life.

Will stumbled through the apartment like that, knocking over DVDs, CDs, and what looked to be an entire tower of graphic novels, but Kenny wasn't getting down for anything in the world. He clung to Will like a magnet at true north, kissing his neck, nibbling on his jaw, and making desperate little noises in his ear.

"It's only been a day," Will panted as he lowered Kenny onto a rather lumpy mattress.

"Don't care," Kenny mumbled, shoving his jeans down to his knees and kicking off his shoes. "Too long."

Will took a moment and shoved everything down and up, and in a second he was on top of Kenny, kissing him some more while Kenny finished kicking his pants off. It was probably five seconds total from hitting the mattress to being completely naked, and Kenny still wrapped his limbs around Will like a barnacle, trying desperately to get as much skin contact as possible.

"I was going to come by," Will said between frantic kisses. He pushed his palm against the flat of Kenny's back and pressed Kenny tighter to him before pulling away for a precious moment.

"Do you want me to take it back?" he asked contrarily, and Will smiled in pure joy.

"Hell no! Just, you know, so you didn't think you were out there by yourself."

Kenny's smile grew suddenly shy. "I knew," he mumbled into Will's chest. "I knew. I'm just stupid about trusting…."

"Less talking, more kissing!" Will demanded, and Kenny's grin was swallowed by another kiss that went on and on and on.

With a little wiggle and some impetus, Kenny rolled Will onto his back and slid down, kissing his chest and his shoulders as he went. He sat on Will's cock and ground hard, frotting back and forth and wanting more.

"Lube, Will. Where's your lube?"

"Under the pillow," Will told him, bucking up against the friction.

Kenny stopped and squinted at him. "What's it doing there?"

Will didn't stop thrusting, but his cheeks turned pink. "You know, I'm here alone a lot in the day."

For a moment Kenny's eyes rolled back in his head and all he could see was an internal slideshow of Will jacking off. "Nungh!"

"Kenny, *focus*!" Will begged.

Kenny took pity, reached under the pillow, and came back with a jumbo bottle of lubricant—that was half-empty.

"But… didn't I get you one of these, like—"

Will grabbed his hips and thrust hard, his ridge catching on Kenny's little pucker. "Twenty-eight years, Kenny," Will panted. "Twenty-eight years thinking sex was for the lucky and the brave. Then I find out I can close my eyes, think of you, and become a frickin' god—now c'mon and make me a god!"

Kenny fumbled with the flip top. The lube was cool on his fingers when he lifted himself and greased Will up, a part of him wanting to stop and laugh in absolute glee and a part of him too turned on to care. He closed the bottle and dropped it on the comforter, then lifted up again and positioned Will just… so….

He slid down slowly, remembering the first time they'd done this and how everything had been new and bright and even the pleasure had hard, sharp edges.

Will groaned from his toes, and suddenly Kenny thought the world was just that bright and sharp and brilliant again, because *ah*, didn't Will feel good all straight and hard inside him. And this *wasn't* the first time, wasn't even the fifth or sixth time, and Will had the experience to hold Kenny's hips still some more and to control the movement while Kenny just hung on for the ride.

"Ahh," Kenny sighed, fulfilled, overwhelmed by how right this was.

Will arched up off the bed and palmed the back of Kenny's head forward until they could kiss. "Good?" Will asked breathlessly.

"God." Kenny was so *full*! He moaned and wiggled and thought about the *size* of the thing inside him. "So good… Will…."

Will rolled over then, because he was good at topping. While Kenny was still scrambling for purchase, he grabbed Kenny's thighs and hauled them both to the edge of the bed so he could stand up.

And then he proceeded to fuck the holy hell out of Kenny with a raw, powerful, possessive, you're-mine-dammit pounding that left Kenny breathless, helpless, gasping and incoherent. Will fumbled for his hand, and for a moment their fingers laced before Will wrapped Kenny's fingers around his own cock and thrust like a train piston until Kenny saw stars. His rim was stretched to burning, and Will's cock was pounding his gland like a giant pounded a kid's trampoline.

"*Ungh*... gonna... gonna... can't...."

"*Come!*" Will thundered, and the command in his voice, the absolute authority, washed Kenny's vision in black and blew an EMP of nuclear ice through his skin, annihilating him in orgasm.

Come-come-shudder-shudder-*come*!

Will roared above him, and Kenny opened his eyes in time to watch him, head thrown back, cords in his neck straining, as he erupted in climax.

For a brilliant flash, every sensation was clear: the dull throbbing in Kenny's still-spurting cock, the *major* throbbing in his distended body, the smell of their sweat, of his semen, and the feeling of Will's fingers pressing into the tops of Kenny's thighs. And through that, all Kenny saw was Will, lost in sex, almost angry with wanting. Wanting *Kenny*.

Will's entire body trembled, and he dropped Kenny's thighs and fell forward, sliding out. Always, always, that moment came too soon. He held himself on his forearms and panted, smiling a little and nuzzling Kenny's temple. Kenny closed his eyes and traveled his hands from Will's chest to shoulders to the back of his neck.

Will eventually flopped to the side and extended his arm. Kenny scooched up and laid his sweaty head on Will's sweatier shoulder.

"Move in with me," Kenny said when he could talk. "I'll beg if I have to."

"Yeah," Will said. "Okay."

And then Kenny rolled over to his side and rested his chin on Will's chest—and took his courage into both hands. "And please, for me, think about working on your business instead of teaching. I want you to be happy. I don't care how much money you make. I can make my own rent—I can't be really happy without a good man to share my home."

Will grimaced. "I'll think about it," he said quietly. "I'm not going to turn down the job just yet."

Kenny swallowed and nodded. "That's fair." He closed his eyes then and realized he'd slept like hell the night before. "Nap," he murmured. "Then we can pack."

"Nap, shower, food, and sex," Will said after him, and his voice sounded as groggy as Kenny felt. "And maybe go to your house and plan sometime in the middle. If we don't feed your cat, we'll find her suspended from the ceiling."

"And pissing on my clothes," Kenny agreed, smiling. It was like Will could read his mind. A good trait in a boyfriend—and the best thing about it was that he cared enough to do it.

"You can meet my mom on Sunday," Will mumbled, and Kenny's eyes brimmed a little, even as he fell asleep.

Something really horrible was going to have to happen to make up for all this good.

THE DANCE ended, and Will gazed into Kenny's dark-blue eyes, feeling a little stupid.

"What?" Kenny asked, and Will remembered the way he'd cried at the wedding itself. Will had known, even from the beginning, that Kenny would be a crier. He liked to act like he had it all together, but his heart was tender.

Will shook his head. "I like weddings," he said, very carefully not saying the things he was thinking. "I like you in them."

Kenny's whole face brightened, and then….

It fell again.

Will bit back a sigh. He couldn't hope a little bit? After the past nine months? But that was okay. Will had a plan for that too.

Right then, the music changed from "I Will Find You" to Dar Williams's "The Ocean." A delicately manicured finger tapped Will's shoulder. "I'm sorry, Kenny" came a warm, familiar voice from behind him. "Can a mother dance with her boy?"

Kenny rested his cheek on Will's chest, an unconscious gesture of possession that Will sort of treasured. He wasn't sure when he'd become Kenny's rock, but he loved that he was.

But Kenny was also a very nice boy underneath all of the savvy he'd worn those first couple of months. "Of course, Mrs. Lafferty—"

"Anne," she said gently. Kenny's mom still made Will call her Mrs. Scalia, but he'd only seen her twice in the last year, so that was okay. Kenny and Will saw Will's mom pretty much once a week. She liked dropping by in the evenings sometimes with plants from Aunt Cara for Kenny's yard, and they'd usually feed her since she hated cooking for herself.

"Of course, Anne," Kenny said, and Will could feel the warmth of his blush through his bright-turquoise wedding suit.

Will kissed his cheek and then turned to his mom, who said, "Save a dance for me too, okay, Kenny?"

Kenny grinned quick and brilliant, and he sauntered off, probably to get more cake before they boxed it up for the evening. It was getting close to ten o'clock, and the dancing was still in force, but the people with kids (including the much put-upon Ashley, who had gone home with her very tired-looking mother) had drifted home once the buffet was put away and the patio lights went up around the yard.

Will took his mom's hand and wrapped his other arm around her waist, very much unlike how he'd danced with Kenny, and grinned.

"Are they happy?" he asked, remembering his mom's surprise when Cara had come out and just sort of announced the wedding with Nina.

"They're perfect," his mom said, smiling guilelessly up at him. "I set the flowers up. Does he suspect?" Her voice dropped to a stage whisper, and he winced, trying not to look behind him to see if Kenny had heard. *Nothing* would make him look more suspicious than doing that in the middle of the dance floor.

"Sh!" Will hushed in spite of himself. "Mom!"

She laughed low, and it sounded burbling and happy and confident. No man in her life, but Will was starting to realize that maybe she wouldn't be looking for one of those for a while.

"You'll have to let me know how he reacts. I thought the—" Will's frantic shushing made her laugh again. "I thought the shiny thing was a nice touch!" she said hurriedly and then collapsed giggling in her son's arms, all dance rhythm forgotten. The final strains of "The Ocean" faded, and Will looked up in time to see Kenny standing by the dance floor with a little box of cake in his hands.

He kissed his mom's cheek and said, "Thanks, Mom," quietly before turning to Kenny. "I'll take that and say our good-byes," Will told them. "You two have the last dance."

He took the box from Kenny, happy that it seemed so solid because he was looking forward to more cake—it had sort of a dreamy amaretto vanilla frosting, and, well, leftover wedding cake would make an appropriate breakfast.

He hoped.

Cara and Nina were still dancing, and Will waited until Cara saw him and opened her arms for a solid hug. She'd long since discarded her suit jacket, and her white sleeveless blouse was so close to something she'd worn when he was a kid that he felt a sudden poignancy to the moment.

This was his aunt Cara, whom his father had never really approved of but whom Will's mother had always adored.

"Be happy," he said as she hugged him tightly, and he knew that she was probably misting over, because that was what people did at weddings.

"I plan to. You too."

"I've got the same plan," he said, and she pulled back and winked at him.

"You'll have to let Nina help with it," she said, and Nina cuddled in under her arm and grinned at him, obviously deliriously happy. "I don't think once was enough."

"Well, it was plenty of times to do it for *me*," Nina corrected, kissing Cara on the cheek, "but I wouldn't mind *planning* it all over again."

Will agreed, said his final good-byes, and then went to fetch Kenny.

Now that it was time to go home and see what Kenny had to say about all these plans, his stomach was all butterflies and gerbils on wheels. His entire life was so very different now. He just couldn't imagine it without Kenny.

And the moment this had dawned on him had come so suddenly out of the September blue.

CHOOSE YOUR WEAPON

"I SHOULD make something else," Kenny said, looking at the covered bowl of Thai basil curry salad in his hands. "She won't like this."

"Kenny, we're *here*. On *time*. And my mother thinks I'm *never* on time—can we just run with this?"

From the passenger seat, Kenny glared at him with agony in his eyes. Will thought he should probably turn the car off, but it was still a hundred gazillion degrees outside, and Kenny looked like he was going to bolt.

"But I'm not dressed right. You said cargo shorts, but that can't be right."

"Hundred. And. Five. Kenny, it's 105 degrees outside. Can we not quibble about cargo shorts and T-shirts?"

"You were going to wear a tank top!" Kenny accused, and Will grunted. Kenny had called it a wifebeater and refused to step foot out the door until Will changed.

"I was *going* to be comfortable visiting my mother. I do this every weekend."

"Yes, but this is the weekend you're moving in with your gay lover, and I need to not look skeezy."

Will ignored the fact that they'd been too busy having sex to even start packing, and went with a laugh. "Kenny, baby, you have *never* looked skeezy. I met you in your *boxer shorts* and we were picking dildos up from the middle of the road, and you were still all class."

Kenny glared in pure outrage, and Will thought maybe that wasn't the best memory he could have brought up. "Please—*please*—tell me your mother doesn't know that story."

Will held up two sober fingers in the time-honored pledge. "As God is my witness, I did not tell my mother I met you picking up dildos in the middle of the road. Now can I turn off the car?"

Kenny's outrage had gone shiny-eyed, and Will sighed. He put the car in park and set the brake, then palmed the back of Kenny's head until their lips met. He'd found Kenny sort of liked it when he got all he-man, so he put some authority into this kiss, made Kenny open his mouth, thrust his tongue in, and kissed like they were at home and the bed was just down the hall.

"Nungh," Kenny said when he pulled back, and Will grinned and tapped his cheek.

"Feel better?"

"No. Now I feel all sexed."

"Good. You relax after sex. That's what we need here. Mom's going to have a basic lunch. Ham sandwiches. Thai basil salad will be awesome. Remember what she told me when I came out?"

"No. I have no idea, you never told me."

"She said, 'I'm glad—you didn't seem to like women, and I don't like to think of you lonely.'"

For a breath, the only sound was the Oldsmobile pumping toxins into the environment. Kenny smiled, still a little bright-eyed, but steadier. "You *were* pretty lonely when I found you."

Will nodded. "Yeah. And now I'm not. See? Will's mommy loves him, and she will love Kenny too, and we can go have salad and get out of this ozone-destroying monster vehicle."

Kenny looked around him like he was just seeing the Oldsmobile for the first time. "You should get a smart car," he said, nodding like that was going to happen *right now*.

"Yeah, Kenny. I'll make it a priority. You know, though, maybe some lunch with my mom first?"

Kenny smiled gamely and unlatched his seatbelt. Will finally, *finally* turned off the car.

Will's mom greeted them at the door. Then she promptly took the salad from Kenny, gave it to Will to set down, and hugged Kenny for all she was worth, following it up with a kiss on the cheek.

Kenny smiled weakly. "Hi, Mrs. Lafferty. It's really nice to meet you."

Will's mom laughed and pinched his cheek. "Oh honey—it's so nice of you to pretend that it is. Will told me you were scared to death."

Kenny was so stressed he didn't even bother to glare. "Little bit, yeah," he admitted. He pulled self-consciously at his eyeball-zapping-green polo shirt, tucked neatly into a trim pair of bright-blue shorts. "I, uhm, I don't know if I've ever met parents... erm, parent before."

Anne Lafferty's laughter made a soft, burbling sound, and as Will set the salad down on the table, he thought that it had always made him happy. Maybe it would have that effect on Kenny as well.

"Well, consider me honored—"

"Mom, this is an awful lot of food—who else is coming? Wait"— Will saw the fresh tomato and pepper salad and a neat assortment of cubed melons—"is Aunt Cara coming?"

Will squirmed as his mom gave him a mock glare. "You couldn't let me finish?"

"Sorry, Mom," he said dutifully, but he spoiled the meekness by winking at Kenny, who, blessed of blesseds, actually smiled.

"Well, I was going to say that your aunt Cara and her new *girl*friend are in the backyard."

"Oh!" Will was excited to see Cara—she'd like Kenny, he was sure of it. Then, as what his mother said sank in: "Oh...."

Will's mother raised her eyebrows with in an indulgent smile.

"*Ooohhhh....*" Because all of that gossip about Cara and her assistant was finally paying off.

Mom nodded. "Yeah. I think it was news to everybody except us. It was certainly news to Cara. But"—and she grinned, delighted as a schoolgirl—"they're so happy together. And we can say we told you so!"

Will grinned back. "God, it's good to be right!"

His mom grimaced playfully. "As we would *not* have been when we were thinking about setting the two of you up. It's just as well you were—"

"Not enthusiastic," Will supplied drily, and Kenny snorted. As they were talking, Kenny took the opportunity to move subtly but possessively into Will's personal space. Will understood: *This is mine. I know he was yours, but I've claimed him.* Will spoke fluent Kenny by now. It was a language of many subtle nuances.

"So did you tell her I was bringing Kenny?" Will asked, thinking about how important it was, suddenly, that his family knew, saw them as a couple, felt Kenny in his life.

His mom laughed like she knew what he was thinking. "I'm sure she's as excited about you as you are about her."

And at that moment, Cara walked in, her curly gray-and-brown hair pulled back into an escaping ponytail, her wide, freckled face open and smiling. She was pulling a woman behind her by the hand, saying, "C'*mon*, Nina—these are really nice people. Besides, you heard her— Will's here with his *boyfriend*."

And Nina rounded the corner, smiling hesitantly.

Kenny smiled at them both and stepped forward. "Hi, I'm Kenny. Will's boyfriend. Pleased to meet you!" But Cara wasn't having any of that.

She rushed Will and gave him a familiar hug, smelling like sweat and earth and like his second mom.

"Oh my God, kiddo! You look so damned happy!"

Will hugged her back gratefully. "You too," he said, and he closed his eyes. It was an odd, sideways sort of blessing, but he thought he was going to be very, very happy to meet the girl he'd never been set up with.

THE MEETING with Kenny's parents did not go quite as smoothly.

"So you're queer too?"

Will tried not to let his mouth swing open. Kenny's brother was an older, taller, *thicker*, more muscular version of Kenny—he was like Kenny on steroids. For a really, really, brain-shrinkingly long time.

"Well, I am if I'm sleeping with your brother," Will said, nodding slowly, hoping Joey would get it without getting ugly about it.

"You don't look gay," Joey said suspiciously.

Will blinked. Well, that was new. "Maybe I'm just really, really happy inside," Will responded with a bright smile.

Joey's admittedly handsome face—planes and angles and an intriguing nose and chin divot, much like Kenny's, only supersized—managed a disgusted expression.

"You're a smartass like Kenny," he grunted, and Will actually laughed.

"Yeah, well, we keep each other amused."

"I don't even want to know about that shit. Man, that's gross." Joey presented his refrigerator-sized back to Will and stalked off to the other side of the yard. The heat had let off a little, and Kenny's parents had little misters all over their porch and spacious backyard—complete with a built-in pool with its own patio in the back corner—so the grassy space in the middle with the militarily ordered flower beds along the edges stayed pretty comfortable.

In fact, it was a whole lot more comfortable over on the porch side of the yard. At the far side of the yard, by the pool, Joey and his two boys with military haircuts and their prim mother (also with a military haircut, but girl style) sort of glared at Will from the spot of shade under the one umbrella.

Will smiled gamely back.

He heard a noise behind him, and Kenny and his mother came through the screen door, each one bearing a tray of buns and condiments, which they put on a picnic table much like Will's mom's.

It was a comforting similarity, and it helped dispel some of the discomfort caused by the pristinely white two-story house and the *Better Homes and Gardens* yard.

Will had dressed up a little—a button-down shirt with his cargo shorts—and Kenny had worn about the same thing. Kenny had also slicked Will's hair back, added a little product, and caught the place under his ear where he frequently missed when he shaved. (He'd had no idea he did this, but Kenny told him it looked like he had a random caterpillar on his face sometimes. Good-*bye*, self-confidence.)

Kenny's mother was wearing a casual shell/skirt set out of a Macy's catalogue, in coordinating colors of khaki and soft rose. It was stunning. Her perfectly dyed and coiffed—yes, coiffed!—blonde hair was pulled up into a chignon, and she wore pearls. For a picnic. Will would have bet her flats were probably from the "picnic" section of the catalogue. Kenny's father, who was standing at the grill after waving Will off, wore khaki slacks with a belt and a khaki-green polo shirt, tucked in.

Will was starting to get Kenny's dress sense. He was always wearing a neat little outfit—probably because he'd had to, growing up—but *his* neat little outfit sparkled and danced with colors that he was *not* going to get from the ecru-and-khaki house that sat behind them.

Kenny's brother and his wife were wearing OD green and khaki. His sons were wearing plain blue T-shirts.

It was starting to give Will the creeps.

So when he saw Kenny coming through the door with his tray after sort of a sheepish "Let me go help Mom" moment, Will was relieved as all hell.

"Here, let me help you!" Even *Will* heard the desperation in his own voice.

"Sorry my brother's a douchemonkey," Kenny said, allowing Will to take a plate of pickles and onions off the tray and set it on the table. "Did you offer to help my dad grill?"

Kenny *had* tried to give Will a heads-up, after all.

"Yeah. He said he didn't need the help."

Kenny grunted. "Dad, let Will help grill—he's good at it."

Will glared at him. "How would you know that?" he hissed, although he'd grilled at his mom's house and he wasn't bad. He didn't burn anything, if that's what it took to be allowed at the man's table.

"Because you're good at everything, and it doesn't matter—Dad's not going to let you near the grill anyway."

"Stop trying to put Will to work," Mrs. Scalia said with a smile. "Come here, Will, and help me set the table."

Will looked at her sharply and saw that she appeared to be unaware of the irony, and one more piece of the Kenny puzzle fell into place. Kenny, with his sharp sense of irony, would have largely assumed nobody would get him.

Well, that was good news for *Will*, who had understood him from "Hence, beer."

Will had always gotten along with his teachers—it was one of the reasons he wanted to be one—so he was right on that whole "suck up to the mom" thing. He set napkins—the nice lineny paper ones—in the little holders next to the thick paper plates, and made sure there was a water glass next to every plate.

He finished the simple task and looked up into Mrs. Scalia's smiling face. She had tiny pixie-ish features, while Mr. Scalia had a blunt, wide, prototypical masculine face, and Will was sort of glad Kenny had gotten her nose and cheekbones.

Joey did not attract him *at all*.

"Nicely done, Will. You must be a joy to your mother."

Oh geez—if that wasn't the classic teacher response. Suddenly Will felt like a big awkward middle schooler again, and he blessed Kenny for not exposing him to this before he'd turned in his apartment key.

"Well," he replied, feeling lame, "I *do* mow her lawn."

"And ours," Kenny supplied perkily. "His mom and aunt Cara even helped us with the flower beds in the back."

"Don't interrupt, Kenny. I'm talking to Will."

Kenny met his eyes in the classic "Dude, I tried!" grimace, and then Will was back on the barbecue, without even some turkey-burger-scented smoke to make the whole thing feel better.

"So, Will, I understand you're a teacher." Her practiced smile invited him to finish that thought.

"Yes, I actually *have* a job lined up for fall semester, but, uhm." He looked at Kenny again, who reassured him with a look of sympathetic patience. "I'm still debating whether or not to take it."

"Really? Why wouldn't you take a job?" Suddenly that teacher's serenity seemed to be penetrated by real curiosity, which relieved him mightily.

"Kenny, uhm, doesn't really believe I'm public-school material," he said apologetically and inwardly winced when he saw Mrs. Scalia turning toward her son with reproof.

"Kenny! Why would you say such a thing?"

Kenny, bless him, stood his ground. "Will's like me, Mom," he said almost defiantly. "He doesn't really fit in the public education box."

Will was suddenly subject to the gimlet glare of a veteran battle-ax, and Mrs. Scalia's position at the table even cut him off from Kenny's sympathetic glances. *Thanks a lot, Kenny. You couldn't have seen that bus coming?*

"He looks perfectly average to me," she said, and Will wasn't sure if that was a good thing.

"He's *not* average," Kenny said passionately. "He's *superlative*. He's *amazing*. He's way too fantabulous for school."

Will watched that teacher's mouth compress, and he cringed, and then something complex and soft happened around Mrs. Scalia's eyes. "Okay," she said simply. "I'll take your word for it, Kenny. But remember, it's hard to pay the bills without a job."

"Oh, he has a job!" Kenny said excitedly. "He's a web designer and—" He swallowed and looked embarrassed. "Tell them, Will."

Will smiled greenly and started talking about website designing, which really, when he thought about it, was a *lot* less interesting than talking about teaching, even if it was more exciting to do sometimes. While he spoke, Joey came and helped Mr. Scalia with the grill, and Mrs. Joey and the two boys moved from their chilly remove to sit at the table. Kenny's mom continued to grill him. Income, business expansion—she asked it *all*.

And then it happened. The subject. The "What happened to your *last* teaching job?" subject.

They were seated around the table by this time, and Will had just chomped down on an *outstanding* turkey burger, which he'd decked out with jalapeños, since they were an option, as well as tomatoes, pickles, grilled onions, and Thousand Island dressing. Kenny's mom did a hamburger bar *right*—but that didn't mean Will wasn't caught flat-footed.

"Mm gob frd fr tmmin Hrrm Pommr."

Kenny burst out laughing and turned to him with a napkin. "She'll let you eat first, precious," he said kindly. "But don't worry—

I'll take this one." He turned to his mom. "He was working at a conservative church school and he let the students read Harry Potter in their spare time."

Mrs. Scalia grimaced. "Oh, honey—you didn't even have a union to protect you!"

Will swallowed the last of his bite. "I am aware," he said drily.

"Why would you do that?" Joey asked from across the table. He'd been largely silent—and, well, productive. He was probably on his third burger by now, while Will was still on his first. Given that Will had five inches and probably forty pounds on him, Will was impressed.

"Why would I what?" Will asked, wanting another bite of his burger.

"Why would you risk your job teaching some stupid fantasy book?"

"Because alternative universe literature promotes critical thinking, imagination, empathy, and creative problem solving. Children who are fluent in fiction are more able to interpret nonfiction and are better at understanding things like basic cause and effect, sociology, politics, and the impact of historical events on current events. Many of our technological advances were imagined by science fiction writers before the tech became available to create them, and many of today's inventors were inspired by science fiction and fantasy to make a world more like the world in the story. Many of today's political conundrums were anticipated by science fiction writers like Orwell, Huxley, and Heinlein, and sci-fi and fantasy tackle ethical problems in a way that allows people to analyze the problem with some emotional remove, which is important because the high emotions are often what lead to violence. Works like Harry Potter tackle the idea of abuse of power and—"

Will stopped himself and swallowed.

Everybody at the table, including Kenny, was staring at him in openmouthed surprise.

"Anyway," he said before taking a monster bite of his cooling hamburger on a sudden attack of nerves, "iss goomfer umf."

"It's good for us," Kenny translated, sounding a little stunned.

Will couldn't look away from his hamburger. Oh God. Kenny's initiation into the extended family had been *easy* compared to this. He swallowed the bite in two gulps and then looked around the table sheepishly.

"Sorry. I, uhm, got a little passionate."

Joey and his family looked blank—they were probably still back on Will's second sentence. But Mrs. Scalia and her husband were both eyeing him thoughtfully.

"Too fantabulous for school," Mrs. Scalia repeated and then looked at her son. "Kenny, I think you might be right." Then she turned to Kenny's brother. "So, Joey, I understand you're trying for another one? Think you'll get a girl this time?"

Joey turned red and started to stammer, and Will let out a real breath for the first time in about five minutes. Next to him, Kenny patted his thigh.

"Sorry," Will muttered under the table chatter, and Kenny set his burger down long enough to kiss Will's shoulder in blessing.

"You're so damned brilliant," he said fervently. "Don't let them give you any shit about making money, sweetheart—I think you just impressed the hell out of them."

"Kenny, did you just swear at the dinner table?" Mrs. Scalia asked, because damn, she must still have her teacher ears on.

"Sorry, Mom!" Kenny sang, and then he picked his burger up with a little wink at Will. He was right—Will *did* eventually get the grilling about whether he could help with the bills and not take advantage of their son's generosity, but since Will worried the same thing, he didn't mind so much.

They were just looking after their son, and Will was all for that. Anyone looking after Kenny had the same priorities he did.

A MONTH later, as a broiling August faded into a sapphire September blue morning, Will waved to Kenny from the porch as Kenny left for work. Kenny kissed him on the cheek before he walked to the car and said, "Don't worry so much about cleaning house, okay? We can both do that. You're working your ass off—don't think I don't see it."

Will smiled sheepishly. He was having trouble remembering that he *worked* from home. He'd garnered enough new clients to make what he'd made teaching, and that was pretty awesome, but even better, he'd had time to work on the website for *Terra'nair: The Chronicles of Calandra.* They had almost a complete graphic novel ready, and most of their pages uploaded. They hoped to get people hooked on the first chapter of the graphic novel and then to start producing merchandise. If they made enough money on the merchandise, they would self-publish the novel and start selling copies at the next convention. It was… it was *amazing* that they would be doing this.

Will woke up every morning with Kenny in his arms (and Princess the cat swishing her tail over his face), wondering how exactly he'd managed to live this sort of amazing life—but he knew.

He had taken a leap of faith.

He'd struggled with that decision—it had been brutal. After dinner with Kenny's parents, they'd started unpacking his apartment and sorting stuff to throw away, and… well. Memories.

The file of student assignments from his first student-taught class, notes from kids from his first short-lived job—hell, the forbidden results of the dinosaur dioramas he'd had the fifth graders from Blessed Hymn Elementary do. He'd kept all of them, because he'd loved getting them, and as he'd prepared to stack them all into the box of things to throw away, his heart stuttered.

"What?" Kenny looked up from uploading his CDs into the iTunes cloud so they could put the actual discs into storage with Will's furniture.

"I really loved getting these," he said, looking at the rather pathetic pieces of cardboard, paper-mache, and glue. "I mean, the kids really loved doing them, and I felt like I was doing something important."

Kenny stopped and stood up, his hands moving restlessly and helplessly at his sides. "I'll bet you're an amazing teacher," he said simply. "You know, you could go back. There's nothing wrong with the job, Will. Just…." Kenny swallowed. "I mean, I met you, and you were so sad. The job… it *rejected* you. Do you think I'm not mad at it? It hurt you before I met you."

Will sighed, gazing sightlessly into the box. He got angry every time any sort of political bill involving teachers came up. He voted to raise his taxes at every opportunity, because he believed in education. But when he hadn't been at the private school, his classroom had been overfilled. Thirty-five kids that age stuffed into a classroom—it had been like wrestling grunion. When they got a little older, that included the sex hormones too. He'd watched kids who were perfectly capable slide lower and lower in their abilities because nobody could get to them—not him, not any of the volunteers. There were just too many of them, and they needed too much.

"I was good at it," he said, feeling a little empty. "I *was* good at it."

"You're still good at it," Kenny said. With jerky movements he moved around the boxes and the coffee table and hovered near Will's shoulder. "I don't want you to quit because you're not good at it."

"Then—"

Kenny rested his hand on Will's bicep and squeezed lightly. "You're just... you have so much talent, Will—"

"But teaching used to be considered a talent," Will protested.

Kenny sighed.

"You're right. It should be. Teachers should be paid a living wage, and they should be given reasonable expectation of privacy, and they should be given input into what they teach. But they're *not*. I've been listening to my mom bitch about these things for years—but the district next to the one she worked in just gave their entire staff a 13 percent pay cut, retroactive, by cutting the number of days they teach."

Will wrinkled his nose. He'd heard about that. It seemed the height of folly—the government kept threatening to pay teachers based on student achievement and then cutting the number of days they had in which to achieve *anything*. It was enough to give him acid reflux, or an ulcer, or just a serious case of political rage—but....

"Money isn't why I love it," he whispered.

Kenny rubbed his back in gentle little circles. "Then maybe go back and do it when money isn't an issue."

Will put the last assignment in the big cardboard box and stroked a plastic dinosaur absently. "That thing we're working on—it's really good. I mean, teenagers are going to love it, right?"

Kenny nodded. "Middle schoolers too. It's... you did a really good job with the plot arc, Will. The dialog is funny—"

"Your drawings are phenomenal," Will said loyally.

Kenny shook his head. "We're not talking about me. We're talking about you and how you're not... I don't know. Giving up. Selling out. You can volunteer at a shelter or a mentor program. You can do comic-book workshops for kids—there's a lot of different ways you can not leave this behind you, Will. I just... I...."

Kenny trailed off unhappily, and Will sighed too. Suddenly Kenny leaned up and kissed his cheek. "I love you. Does that help? I'll love you if you go back to teaching and stay poor, and I'll love you if you have some faith that this thing we do, it'll be worth it. I'll love you if your business fails and you have to start from scratch. I. Love. You. You taught me to have faith that all men aren't just after the shiny. Maybe you should have some faith that you're not just dependable teacher guy. You're shiny too."

Will smiled a little. "Good speech," he said softly, leaning his chin against Kenny's forehead.

"Yeah, well, I've been practicing it for a while in my head."

Will laughed slightly. Wordlessly he shoved the box to the corner with all of the trash bags and turned back to sorting through the detritus on his bookshelf.

The next morning, before they took the rest of Will's stuff to the storage facility with his old furniture, he walked into Kenny's bedroom with his cell phone and called his new principal.

"Hey, Dr. Hanline, I was wondering—what's your school's policy on having a GSA?"

"Uhm, well, given the climate in our local constituency, I think that's probably—"

Will tuned him out. It was that simple. He waited until the man who was going to be his boss petered out, and said, "I'm sorry, sir. I've had a better offer. Please find someone else to fill my spot."

He ended the call and threw himself facedown on the bed, still wondering what the hell he was doing.

Kenny had been in the middle of putting on his shorts when Will started the phone call, and now he finished putting on his belt and threw himself on the bed next to Will.

"Congratulations," Will said, feeling lost. "Your new boyfriend is now an unemployed freeloader—your parents must be very proud."

"Screw 'em," Kenny told him, kissing his shoulder. "I get to live with you. I win."

And that was what Kenny had continued to say even as they set Will up in the guest room with his desk and his office supplies and Princess, who kept sleeping on his chair whenever he got up for water.

So by this sunny, still-hot day in the beginning of September, Will had a routine. He worked for a few hours, rode his bike or worked out, came home, and worked for a few more hours. It was harder than it sounded—things like grocery shopping or cleaning the house or working on the lawn beckoned, and Will had to fight the compulsion, still live in his veins, to *do something* that wasn't his actual job. His actual job, whether it was setting up websites for clients or setting up the site for him and Kenny, was still too much fun to consider work.

He was still a little bit in awe.

And a little sad. As he waved Kenny good-bye, he saw a familiar figure trudging along the sidewalk and getting ready to walk across the street.

"Mr. Lafferty?" the kid asked, looking at Will in disbelief. "Why weren't you teaching at the end of the year?"

Will shrugged. "Hey, Carter. They didn't like the things I taught," he said kindly. "But I missed you guys!"

"Are you not teaching anymore at *all*?" Carter responded. "What are you doing *here*?"

Will gave a little half smile and decided in for a penny, in for a pound. "I live here now. I moved in with my boyfriend before the end of the summer."

Carter's mouth fell open and his eyes glazed over. "Can boys *have* boyfriends?" he asked.

Will fought and lost against a sigh. "God, I hope so," he responded, "'cause mine makes me really happy."

"Huh." Carter turned to cross the street. "That's really weird."

"Have a good school year," Will told him. "Keep an open mind."

Carter waved absently, still chewing his bottom lip as he took advantage of an open spot to cross the street.

For a moment Will was overwhelmed, sad, and depressed, because he wasn't going to be able to change this boy's mind.

Then he remembered he had a project waiting for him, something he thought was worthwhile and interesting, that taught the values of tolerance just like science fiction had *always* been cutting-edge in its espousal of human rights.

New boyfriend, new job, new life.

Not bad for a guy who'd been puzzled while picking dildos off the road.

"NICE WEDDING?" Will asked as they returned from Cara and Nina's wedding, even though he knew the answer.

"Uh-huh," Kenny said absently, looking out the Oldsmobile window. "Haven't seen them since SacAnime—it was nice."

Cara, Nina, and Will's mom had shown up for their first convention. They'd sold half of their stock—and made their table money for the next con in San Francisco. They weren't going to be rich overnight, but they had a good following, with plenty of money to maintain the website and enough to order another printing on their first book and start printing the second one, which they'd finished in the winter. As a side business—one they enjoyed the hell out of—it was a start.

Will thought it was maybe the most fun he'd ever had doing *anything* in his life, and the fact that the web designing business gave him enough time to invest in it made him supremely grateful.

"Yeah, well, we should have them to dinner," Will said practically.

Kenny looked at him, surprised. "Yeah, we should. Can we invite Cam and his family too?"

Will shrugged. He'd met Cam at the Labor Day picnic and had seen him at the Halloween children's function, the office Christmas party, and an Easter-egg hunt. (In a fit of altruism and pity for people like Cam with multiple children, Will and Kenny had volunteered to dye the eggs. Never. Again.) "I don't see why not. We're sort of grown-ups. Don't grown-ups do that?"

Kenny laughed shortly. "Jesus—I'm twenty-seven years old. You'd think I'd remember, right?"

Will drove for a few more minutes in the comfortable silence, then rolled the window down in the Olds and hit the radio. A-ha's "Take on Me" came on, and he started singing, off-key, because he didn't know how else to sing.

A moment later Kenny was singing too, and they sustained that throughout the song. Between the pine and dust of the foothills and the warm, silken air, Will thought it was maybe one of the most beautiful moments of his life.

"So," Kenny said when the song was over, "do you ever think about the whole wedding thing?"

"Yeah, all the time." Will smiled smugly to himself.

"Do you think about it with *me*?" Kenny asked, his voice squeaking at the end of the sentence.

Will—who hadn't been able to hold off for three hours before telling his mother he was gay—would be forever proud of the fact that his voice didn't betray him, not now. "Of course with you," he said, sounding exasperated. "I picture it all the time. You'd have to pick the tuxes, of course, and I wouldn't want it to be too big."

"Maybe in Tahoe," Kenny said, sounding like he really liked the idea. "People get married by the lake."

"Yeah, that sounds nice. Or maybe a con wedding, in cosplay!" They had met a whole bunch of *amazing* vendors as they'd visited various conventions. Those people had known one another, had traveled together, met up in different cities together. They were like the peer group Will had never known he'd wanted. He was afraid Kenny would guffaw, because it was sort of a corny idea, but Kenny was, well,

Will's *mate*, and he wasn't going to laugh at something they'd both loved.

"We could do that! You know, this other story we're thinking of—"

"The one with the two guys?" It was a romance, and if they were lucky, they'd have it produced in time for Bent-Con in November.

"Yeah—we could dress up like our own characters and, you know, make it a thing? People could dress up—it could be a party!"

Will laughed, because even if they decided to host a small wedding with a couple of people at Tahoe, the idea was still appealing. Nina and Cara's wedding had been a party, and everyone had enjoyed the food, the dancing, and the company. He'd never thought about it until tonight, but a wedding really was a gift to the community, wasn't it? It was a celebration—that was *awesome*.

"I don't think my parents would dress up," Kenny said dispiritedly. They had *not* shown up at SacAnime.

Will patted his knee. "Well, they'd be missing out," he said, thinking it was true. "And who knows—maybe Joey's kids will." Because if *anyone* needed a healthy dose of imagination, it was the twin GI Joes who kept visiting Kenny's parents during the holidays.

THEY TALKED the whole way back, planning their imaginary wedding, and for once, Will's luck seemed to hold true, because Kenny didn't ask once who was going to propose to whom.

Will made a deal of hanging back to lock the car when they arrived home, and Kenny walked through the door still talking about *making* his parents dress up, preferably as furries, when he turned on the kitchen light like they always did.

Will got into the room just in time to hear him gasp in surprise.

"Omigod. Oh my *God*. Oh. My. God!"

Will stood behind him and took it all in—because he'd come up with the plan, but his mother had done the execution after he and Kenny had left early to help set up the chairs.

In the center of the table were the requisite dozen roses, for romance, because Will didn't have a whole lot of experience giving flowers, so he went with the classics. In front of the roses was the same kind of bright glass bowl they'd bought for Cara and Nina, except Kenny's was in lime green, because next to deep blue, it was his favorite color. In the bowl was a box—open—with a pair of bright brushed gold rings, the smaller one with a heart next to "William" and the bigger one with a heart next to "Kenny," engraved on the outside of the band.

Next to the box was a giant gold vibrating dildo with a note taped to it.

Kenny clapped his hand over his mouth and looked at Will with dancing, shining eyes.

"Go ahead," Will said, biting his lip. "Read the note."

Kenny's hand shook as he picked up the toy, and he didn't even seem to notice what he was holding when he read the note—carefully written on a thick white embossed piece of paper.

> *Unlike this thing, my love for you will always be shiny. Marry me.*
> *Will.*

The vibrator made a clunk when Kenny dropped it on the table. That clunk was the only sound in the room.

Then Kenny launched himself into Will's arms and just held him tight while their breath roared in Will's ears.

"Yes."